Acclaim for Aimee Bender's

Willful Creatures

"Beautifully told, studded with eye-popping details. . . . Bender
is funny and astonishingly perceptive, especially when it comes
to human emotions."   —*People*

"Prose so animated it seems almost capable of writing itself."
—*The Atlantic Monthly*

"Think of a width of exquisite lace, fashioned by a master ar-
tisan who has thrown away any idea of a previous pattern.
Then think of the thread that makes up that lace as being in-
credibly dense and sturdy and strong. That's what the stories
in this collection resemble."   —*The Washington Post*

"Experimental in the best sense, these stories are at once
risky and self-assured and . . . bitterly funny."
—*New York* magazine

"Bender's stories . . . range in length and voice, floating in the
ethereal space between naturalism and magic realism. . . . This
collection moves along effortlessly, though you will linger in
the 'what' it reveals."   —*San Francisco Chronicle*

"Sublime studies on sorrow, grief, kindness and love." – *Time*

"Each story is laced with a bit of arsenic that curls the tongue and sharpens the breath. Narrative storms—loneliness, suspicion, torture, and death—sweep in and electrocute the landscape with jagged lightening." – *The Believer*

"Aimee Bender has created a series of glisteningly weird miniatures. . . . Bender's vision, with its dark, plucky humor and touches of the bizarre, has the power to make us cringe for our own world." – *Esquire*

"If there's any serious writer going against the stream of realistic short fiction these days it's Los Angeles storymaker Aimee Bender. . . . She moves language the way painters move paint." – *Chicago Tribune*

"The absorbing *Willful Creatures* is full of surprise and dark instruction conveyed with graceful humor. . . . Real and beautiful." – *Bookforum*

"Her imagination packs all the gleaming surreality of a Magritte painting, her wry tone the poker-faced irony of a Haruki Murakami novel, her furious satire the bite of a Lynda Barry cartoon. The stories in *Willful Creatures* delight even as they unsettle." – *Time Out New York*

"Few are as good at sociological surveillance as Aimee Bender. Her brilliance isn't just in picking up on the tiny, whispered actions that stand for our big ideas and giant hang-ups, it's in artfully and stealthily turning them around and feeding them back to us as matter-of-fact human nature."

—Seattle Weekly

"*Willful Creatures* is an essential work that should be required reading for any who delight in deft prose and truly empathetic portraits of the human condition."

—Fort Worth Star-Telegram

"There's strangeness in [Bender's] stories, yet the feelings they draw from readers, after some initial discomfort, are timeless and conventional: From oddness she evokes tenderness, and from her characters' peculiarities (they're often very dark) she produces romance." *—The Arizona Republic*

"They're entertaining and funny and weird, but they're idiosyncratic as hell: they're, well, *Bender's* as much as they are stories, original and probably inimitable, the way Richard Brautigan's stories were back in the day." *—OC Weekly*

"Whether in novel or short-story form, her surreal, fractured fairy-tales leave readers shaken *and* stirred in equal measure."

—Elle

Also by
Aimee Bender

The Girl in the Flammable Skirt
An Invisible Sign of My Own

Aimee Bender

Willful Creatures

Aimee Bender is the author of the short story collection *The Girl in the Flammable Skirt* and the novel *An Invisible Sign of My Own*. Her stories have appeared in *Granta*, *GQ*, *Harper's*, *The Paris Review*, and other magazines, and have been heard on PRI's *This American Life*. She lives in Los Angeles.

Willful Creatures

Stories

Aimee Bender

Anchor Books

A Division of Random House, Inc.

New York

FIRST ANCHOR BOOKS EDITION, AUGUST 2006

Some of the stories in this book were published, in slightly different form, in the following
journals: "Death Watch" in *Dust-Up*; "End of the Line" in *Tin House*; "The Meeting"
and "Motherfucker" in *Fence*; "Debbieland" in *Black Clock*; "Fruit and Words" in
Mid-American Review; "Jinx" in *Bridge, Pushcart Prize Anthology*; "I Will Pick Out Your
Ribs (from My Teeth)" in *Land-Grant College Review*; "Ironhead" in *Joe*; "Job's Jobs" in *LA
Weekly, Other Voices*; "Dearth" in *On the Rocks, KGB Reader*; "The Case of the Salt and
Pepper Shakers" in *McSweeney's*; and "The Leading Man" in *The Paris Review*.

The Library of Congress has cataloged the Doubleday edition as follows:
Bender, Aimee.
Willful creatures : stories / Aimee Bender.–1st ed.
p. cm.
1. Fantasy fiction, American. I. Title.
PS3552.E538447W55   2005
813'.54–dc22
2004065515

Anchor ISBN-10: 0-385-72097-1
Anchor ISBN-13: 978-0-385-72097-7

Book design by Terry Karydes

www.anchorbooks.com

Printed in the United States of America
10 9 8 7 6 5

For

Ardie, Jeanne, and Judith

Contents

Part Three

Willful Creatures

Part One

Death
Watch

Ten men go to ten doctors. All the doctors tell all the men that they only have two weeks left to live. Five men cry. Three men rage. One man smiles. The last man is silent, meditative. Okay, he says. He has no reaction. The raging men, upon meeting in the lobby, don't know what to do with the man of no reaction. They fall upon him and kill him with their bare hands. The doctor comes out of his office and apologizes, to the dead man.

Dang it, he says sheepishly, to his colleagues. Looks like I got the date wrong again.

One can't account for murder or accidents, says another doctor in his bright white coat.

The raging, sad men and the smiling man all leave the office. The smiling man does not know why he is smiling. He just feels relieved. He was suicidal anyway. Now it's out of his hands. The others growl at him, their bare hands blood specked, but the smiler is eerie in his relief, and so they let him be, thinking he might somehow speed up their precious two weeks. The raging men tear out the door first; the crying men follow.

On their way they meet up with a field of cows. The cows are chewing quietly and calmly. The sight of the cows fills the crying men with sadness as they only have two weeks left to look at cows. But the sight of the cows fills the raging men with more rage. After all, why are the cows so calm? Why is it that cows get to remain ignorant of their own death? Why is the sky so blue and peaceful? The raging men run to the cows but the cows don't notice; the cows want, more than anything, just to continue chewing. One raging man collapses in the field and drums it with his fists. The others run and run. The five crying men stand at the fence, crying. Look at the sad and large rage of the doomed men, they think. Who knew a cow was so beautiful? Why was I not a farmer? Why not a field hand? Why an office building?

Back at the office building, the doctors check their notebooks and discover an error. Oops. Only two of the five crying men need to be crying. The other three are in perfect health. The doctors, embarrassed, call up their patients who are by then crying into the arms of their crying wives or lovers or pets.

We have some good news! they say. We made a goof. You seem to be in perfect health. Very sorry about that.

One crying man, new lease on life, moves his family to the countryside where they raise goats.

The other two go back to their regular routines. A close call.

The last raging man still is drumming his fists on the field. His lover calls out into the darkness of the night. The lover understands that his angry man is out there raging against the world again, this is to be expected, but he does not understand why the doctor keeps calling.

The suicidal one is another error, but he is impossible to contact. He has flown by now to Greece and is trying finally to have a relationship. With only a couple of weeks left, he thinks that for once he has a good chance of having someone by his bedside when he dies.

The two remaining crying men die. One with tubes, the other in his own bed. One of the raging men dies, roaring in his bathtub. Another, though not a mistake, still drums that field with his fists. The very energy it takes should drain him dry, but no. He is happily drumming. He drums for weeks and sits up and isn't yet dead. It takes him six months, which he uses to make some angry paintings that are beloved by people in galleries who are unaware that they themselves are angry at all.

The Greek woman sobs when she hears that her wonderful melancholy lover will be dying soon. They do ritual after ritual. Their sex is like castles; it has moats and turrets. If only, thinks the suicidal man, if only I had known for longer how short it all would be.

Everybody says this. They say it for us, the nondying, to remember our daily lives. But we can't fully get it until we're right up in the face of it. Can we get it? It is hard to get. I do not get it. Only the suicidal man gets it here, and his Greek lover with her aquiline nose.

On the morning of the third week, the Greek woman returns to her bedroom with a bouquet of mourning flowers. She has prepared herself on the walk over for the cold body. She can still feel him inside her. In the bedroom, her lover says hello. He feels curiously fine. The Greek woman falls to her knees and calls him a miracle. They have miracle sex, in honor of miracles. But the next day happens the same and both are giddy with joy tinged by the slightest bit of disappointment which they hide behind their love and delight. And then the next day, and soon the sex is not the same as before. No longer a castle, now just a hut. The Greek woman's husband is due back soon anyway, from his voyage to get silk from China. The suicidal man goes to the sea to bathe. Some cows walk by, chewing. He can feel his heart, like the strongest machine, and his deathbedside fading.

He takes the plane back home and gets off at the layover city, a city he does not know. He'd bought himself a return ticket even though he'd assumed, even hoped, he would die in Greece, among clean-washed buildings and simple color contrast that is enough to satisfy everything: White on blue. Yellow on blue. Red on white. He had planned on giving his return ticket to his Greek lover in case she needed to escape her husband and set up a new life in America. She was not thrilled, though, by his generous offer. Thank you, she'd said, but I do not like this television all the time.

The stopover from Athens is in Denver. Not what he pictured. A place he has never been. He grew up elsewhere, not in or by mountains. So, so, so. Let's walk over the streets, he says to himself, and the first FOR RENT sign he sees, he takes. He does everything the minute he thinks it—that is, all except suicide. He does not want to be cheated of his terminal illness.

His illness is not terminal; instead it is temporary. He never speaks to the doctors who try to leave a message but discover that the mechanical lady is now answering his phone. But he figures it out on his own. He thinks possibly he's one of those people who will live forever but when he cuts himself shaving he bleeds so profusely he spells out MORTAL in the sink's basin with his blood. He joins a gym. The world of Denver fills him up with coffee in the morning and walks in the afternoon. He is spending all his money.

Eventually he calls his doctor, because he's too curious. He explains to the secretary how he was told he had two weeks to live and now it's three years later. The doctor, he hears, has died. From guilt perhaps? No. The doctor was in a skiing accident.

You can't account for events like that, he says to himself,

going outside to appreciate the simple color contrast of Colorado: Brown on blue. Green on brown.

It feels like a trade-off, even though it wasn't. He returns to his hometown the next day. There he finds the doctor's wife and life and he seduces her with his depressive charm. He is a good new stepparent. One afternoon the Greek woman shows up on his doorstep. I have left my husband, she says. I miss you my darling and your delicate fingertips.

He is brimming with abundance but it's too late for all of them. When the bomb hits, the doctors shake their heads at each other as their bodies disintegrate.

You can never account, they say, for murder, or for accidents.

They are all, at once, at each other's deathbeds.

End of *the* Line

The man went to the pet store to buy himself a little man to keep him company. The pet store was full of dogs with splotches and shy cats coy and the friendly people got dogs and the independent people got cats and this man looked around until in the back he found a cage inside of which was a miniature sofa and tiny TV and one small attractive brown-haired man, wearing a tweed suit. He looked at the price tag. The little man was expensive but the big man had a reliable job and thought this a worthy purchase.

He brought the cage up to the front, paid with his credit card, and got some free airline points.

In the car, the little man's cage bounced lightly on the passenger seat, held by the seat belt.

The big man set up the little man in his bedroom, on the nightstand, and lifted the latch of the cage open. That's the first time the little man looked away from the small TV. He blinked, which was hard to see, and then asked for some dinner in a high shrill voice. The big man brought the little man a drop of whiskey inside the indented crosshatch of a screw, and a thread of chicken with the skin still on. He had no utensils, so he told the little man to feel free to eat with his hands, which made the little man irritable. The little man explained that before he'd been caught he'd been a very successful and refined technology consultant who'd been to Paris and Milan multiple times, and that he liked to eat with utensils thank you very much. The big man laughed and laughed, he thought this little man he'd bought was so funny. The little man told him in a clear crisp voice that dollhouse stores were open on weekends and he needed a bed, please, with an actual pillow, please, and a lamp and some books with actual pages if at all possible. Please. The big man chuckled some more and nodded.

The little man sat on his sofa. He stayed up late that first night, laughing his high shrill laugh at the late-night shows, which annoyed the big man to no end. He tried to sleep and could not, a wink. At four A.M., exhausted, the big man put some antihistamine in the little man's water-drip tube, so the little man finally got drowsy. The big man accidentally put too much in, because getting the right proportions was no easy feat of mathematical skill, which was not the big man's strong suit anyway, and the little man stayed groggy for three days, slugging around his cage, leaving tiny drool marks on the couch. The big man went to work and thought of the little man with longing all day, and at five o'clock he dashed home, so excited he was to see his little man, but he kept finding the fellow in a state of murk. When the antihistamine finally wore off, the little man awoke with crystal-clear sinuses, and by then had a fully furnished room around him, complete with chandelier and several very short books, including *Cinderella* in Spanish, and his very own pet ant in a cage.

The two men got along for about two weeks. The little man was very good with numbers and helped the big man with his bank statements. But between bills, the little man also liked to talk about his life back home and how he'd been captured on his way to work, in a bakery of all places, by the little-men bounty hunters, and how much he, the little man, missed his wife and children. The big man had no wife and no children, and he didn't like hearing that part. "You're mine now," he told the little man. "I paid good money for you."

"But I have responsibilities," said the little man to his owner, eyes dewy in the light.

"You said you'd take me back," said the little man.

"I said no such thing," said the big man, but he couldn't remember if he really had or not. He had never been very good with names or recall.

After about the third week, after learning the personalities of the little man's children and grandparents and aunts and uncles, after hearing about the tenth meal in Paris and how le waiter said the little man had such good pronunciation, after a description of singing tenor arias with a mandolin on the train to Tuscany, the big man took to torturing the little man. When the little man's back was turned, the big man snuck a needle-thin droplet of household cleanser into his water and watched the little man hallucinate all night long, tossing and turning, retching small pink piles into the corners of the cage. His little body was so small it was hard to imagine it hurt that much. How much pain could really be felt in a space that tiny? The big man slept heavily, assured that his pet was just exaggerating for show.

The big man started taking sick days at work.

He enjoyed throwing the little man in the air and catching him. The little man protested in many ways. First he said he didn't like that in a firm fatherly voice, then he screamed and cried. The man didn't respond so the little man used reason, which worked briefly, saying: "Look, I'm a man too, I'm just a little man. This is very painful for me. Even if you don't like me," said the little man, "it still hurts." The big man listened for a second, but he had come to love flicking his little man, who wasn't talking as much anymore about the art of the baguette, and the little man, starting to bruise and scar on his body, finally shut his mouth completely. His head ached and he no longer trusted the water.

He considered his escape. But how? The doorknob is the Empire State Building. The backyard is an African veldt.

The big man watched TV with the little man. During the show with the sexy women, he slipped the little man down his pants and just left him there. The little man poked at the big man's penis which grew next to him like Jack's beanstalk in person, smelling so musty and earthy it made the little man embarrassed of his own small penis tucked away in his consultant pants. He knocked his fist into it, and the beanstalk grew taller and, disturbed, the big man reached down his pants and flung the little man across the room. The little man hit a table leg. Woke up in his cage, head throbbing. He hadn't even minded much being in the underwear of the big man, because for the first time since he'd been caught, he'd felt the smallest glimmer of power.

"Don't you try that again," warned the big man, head taking up the north wall of the cage entirely.

"Please," said the little man, whose eyes were no longer dewy but flat. "Sir. Have some pity."

The big man wrapped the little man up in masking tape, all over his body, so his feet couldn't kick and there were only little holes for his mouth and his eyes. Then he put him in the refrigerator for an hour. When he came back the little man had fainted and the big man put him in the toaster oven, at very very low, for another ten minutes. Preheated. The little man revived after a day or two.

"Please," he said to the big man, word broken.

The big man didn't like the word please. He didn't like politesse and he didn't like people. Work had been dull and no one had noticed his new coat. He got himself a ticket to Paris with all the miles he'd accumulated on his credit card, but soon realized he could not speak a word of the language and was too afraid of accidentally eating veal brains to go. He did not want to ask the little man to translate for him as he did not want to hear the little man's voice with an accent. The thought of it made him so angry. The ticket expired, unreturned. On the plane, a young woman stretched out on her seat and slept since no one showed up in the seat next to hers. At work, he asked out an attractive woman he had liked for years, and she ran away from him to tell her coworkers immediately. She never even said no; it was so obvious to her, she didn't even have to say it.

"Take off your clothes," he told the little man that afternoon.

The little man winced and the big man held up a bottle of shower cleanser as a threat. The little man stripped slowly, folded his clothing, and stood before the big man, his skin pale, his chest a matted grass of hair, his penis hiding, his lips trembling so slightly that only the most careful eye would notice.

"Do something," said the big man.

The little man sat on the sofa. "What," he said.

"Get hard," said the big man. "Show me what you look like."

The little man's head was still sore from hitting the table leg; his brain had felt fuzzy and indistinct ever since he'd spent the hour in the refrigerator and then time in the toaster oven. He put his hand on his penis and there was a heavy sad flicker of pleasure and behind the absolute dullness of his mind, his body rose up to the order.

The big man laughed and laughed at the erection of his little man, which was fine and true but so little! How funny to see this man as a man. He pointed and laughed. The little man stayed on the sofa and thought of his wife, who would go into the world and collect the bottle caps strewn on the ground from the big people and make them into trays; she'd spend hours upon hours filing down the sharp edges and then use metallic paint on the interior and they were the envy of all the little people around, so beautiful they were and so hearty. No one else had the patience to wear down those sharp corners. Sometimes she sold one and made a good wad of cash. The little man thought of those trays, trays upon trays, red, blue, and yellow, until he came in a small spurt, the orgasm pleasureless but thick with yearning.

The big man stopped laughing.

"What were you thinking about?" he said.

The little man said nothing.

"What's your wife like?" he said.

Nothing.

"Take me to see her," the big man said.

The little man sat, naked, on the floor of his cage. He had changed by now. Cut off. He would have to come back, a long journey back. He'd left.

"See who?" he asked.

The big man snickered. "Your wife," he said.

The little man shook his head. He looked wearily at the big man. "I'm the end of this line for you," he said.

It was the longest sentence he'd said in weeks. The big man pushed the cage over and the little man hit the side of the sofa.

"Yes!" howled the big man. "I want to see your children too. How I love children!"

He opened the cage and took the little floral-print couch into his hand. The little man's face was still and cold.

"No," he said, eyes closed.

"I will torture you!" cried out the big man.

The little man folded his hands under his cheek in a pillow. Pain was no longer a mystery to him, and a man familiar with pain has entered a new kind of freedom. "No," he whispered into his knuckles.

With his breath clouding warmly over his hands, the little man waited, half dizzy, to be killed. He felt his death was terribly insignificant and a blip but he still did not look forward to being killed and he sent waves of love to his wife and his children, to the people who made him significant, to the ones who felt the blip.

The big man played with the legs of the little armchair. He took off the pillow and found a few coins inside the crevices, coins so small he couldn't even pick them up.

He put his face close to the cage of his little man.

"Okay," he said.

Four days later, he set the little man free. He treated him well for the four days, gave him good food and even a bath and some aspirin and a new pillow. He wanted to leave him with some positive memories and an overall good impression. After four days, he took the cage under his arm, opened the front door, and set it out on the sidewalk. Unlocked the cage door. The little man had been sleeping nonstop for days, with only a few lucid moments staring into the giant eye of the big man, but the sunlight soaked into him instantly, and he awoke. He exited the cage door. He waited for a bird to fly down and eat him. Not the worst death, he thought. Usually the little people used an oil rub that was repellent-smelling to birds and other animals, but all of that, over time, had been washed clean off him. He could see the hulking form of the big man to his right, squatting on his heels. The big man felt sad but not too sad. The little man had become boring. Now that he was less of a person, he was easier to get along with and less fun to play with. The little man tottered down the sidewalk, arms lifting oddly from his sides, as if he had wet hands or was covered in paint. He did not seem to recognize his own body.

At the curb, he sat down. A small blue bus drove up, so small the big man wouldn't have noticed it if he hadn't been looking at foot level already. The little man got on. He had no money but the bus revved for a moment and then moved forward with the little man on it. He took a seat in the back and looked out the window at the street. All the little people around him could smell what had happened. They lived in fear of it every day. The newspapers were full of updates and new incidents. One older man with a trim white beard moved across the bus to sit next to the little man and gently put an arm on his shoulder. Together they watched the gray curbs passing by.

On the lawn, the big man thought the bus was hilarious and walked next to it for a block. Even the tires rolled perfectly. He thought how if he wanted to, he could step on that bus and smush it. He did not know that the bus was equipped with spikes so sharp they would drive straight through a rubber sole, into the flesh of the foot. For a few blocks he held his foot over it, watching bus stops come up, signs as small as toothpicks, but then he felt tired and went to the corner and let the bus turn and sat down on the big blue plastic bus bench on his corner made for the big people.

When his bus came, he took it. It was Saturday. He took it to the very end of the line. Here the streets were littered with trash, and purple mountains anchored the distance. Everything felt like it was closing in, and even the store signs seemed too bright and overwhelming. He instantly didn't like it, this somewhere he had never been before, with a different smell, that of a sweeter flower and a more rustic bread. The next bus didn't come for an hour so he began the steady walk home, eyes glued to the sidewalk.

He just wanted to see where they lived. He just wanted to see their little houses and their pets and their schools. He wanted to see if they each had cars or if buses were the main form of transport. He hoped to spot a tiny airplane.

"I don't want to harm you!" he said out loud. "I just want to be a part of your society."

His eyes moved across grasses and squares of sidewalk. He'd always had excellent vision.

"In exchange for seeing your village," he said out loud, "I will protect you from us. I will guard your front gates like a watchdog!" He yelled it into the thorny shadows of hedges, down the gutter, into the wet heads of sprinklers.

All he found was a tiny yellow hat with a ribbon, perched perfectly on the yellow petal of a rose. He held it for a good ten minutes, admiring the fine detail of the handiwork. There was embroidery all along the border. The rim of the hat was the size of the pad of his thumb. Everything about him felt disgusting and huge. Where are the tall people, the fatter people? he thought. Where are the aliens the size of God?

Finally, he sat down on the sidewalk.

"I've found a hat!" he yelled. "Please! Come out! I promise I will return it to its rightful owner."

Nestled inside a rock formation, a group of eight little people held hands. They were on their way to a birthday party. Tremendous warmth generated from one body to the other. They could stand there forever if they had to. They were used to it. Birthdays came and went. Yellow hats could be resewn. It was not up to them to take care of all the world, whispered the mother to the daughter, whose yellow dress was unmatched, whose hand thrummed with sweat, who watched the giant outside put her hat on his enormous head and could not understand the size of the pity that kept unbuckling in her heart.

At the party I make a goal and it is to kiss three men: one with black hair, one with red hair, the third blond. Not necessarily in that order. I'm alone at the party and I have my drink in a mug because by the time I got here, at the ideal moment of lateness, the host had used all her bluish glasses with fluted stems that she bought from the local home-supply store that all others within a ten-block radius had bought too because at some inexplicable point in time, everybody woke up with identical taste. I see two matching sweaters and four similar handbags. It's enough to make you want to buy ugly except other people are having that reaction too and I spot three identically ugly pairs of shoes. There's just nowhere to hide. I know the host here from high-school time and she likes to invite me to things because for one, she feels sorry for me and for two, she finds me entertaining and blushes when I cuss. It's how we flirt.

About half the people here are in couples. I stand alone because I plan on making all these women jealous, reminding them how incredible it is to be single instead of always being with the same old same old except tonight I am jealous too because all their men are seeming particularly tall and kind on this foggy wintery night and one is wearing a shirt a boyfriend of mine used to own with that nubby terry-cloth material recycled from soda cans and it smells clean from where I'm standing, ten feet away, and it's not a good sign when something like a particular laundry detergent can just like that undo you.

From here, against the wall, I can survey the whole living room. TV, couch, easy plant. The walls are covered with pastel posters of gardens by famous painters who rediscovered light and are now all over address books and umbrellas and mugs. Is it really worth it to dead earless van Gogh that his painting now holds some person's catalog of phone numbers? Is that what he wanted when he fought through personal hell to capture the sun in Arles? I used to paint and I would make landscapes that were peaceful and my teacher would stroll through the easels and praise me and say, "What a lovely cornfield, dear," but she never looked hard enough because if you did you would see that each landscape had something bad in it and that lovely was the wrong word to use: I made that cornfield, true, but if you looked closely, there was a glinting knife hanging from each husk. And I made a beach scene with crashing waves and a crescent moon and then this loaded machine gun lying on the sand by a towel; and then I made a mountain town with quaint stores and tall pine trees and people walking around except for that one man wrapped in dynamite walking over to the guy with the cigarette lighter standing by the drinking fountain.

The terrible thing is that the teacher never figured it out. And she saw all three paintings. She actually thought the guy in dynamite was wearing some strange puffy suit and that the corn was just very glinty. She said the machine gun was a nice kite. When the evaluation sheets came around, I said she was useless and should be fired.

The couples are shifting positions and I'm ready now and I find that redhead first. Lucky for me he is drunk already and sitting in a chair with pretzels and he's talking to no one because he's on break from being social because he is so drunk. I saunter over and ask him to help me look for my purse in the bedroom. "I lost my purse," I say to him. "Help." He blinks, eyelids heavy with the eye shadow of alcohol, and then he follows me into the bedroom which is covered with people's items: twenty-five coats and half as many purses. I am rich but I consider stealing some of the stuff because they are so trusting, these people, and I feel like wrecking their trust. But where would I stash a coat? We are looking around for my make-believe purse because I don't use a purse at all; when I go out, I just carry keys and slip one one-hundred-dollar bill into the arch of my shoe and let the night unroll from there. We're mumbling in the bedroom and I pretend I'm drunker than I am and then I ask him, right there, among all the coats, if he thinks I'm pretty. His eyes are bleary and he smiles and says, "Yeah, yeah." We're standing by the bed, and I lean over and I kiss him then, really gentle because at any minute he could throw up all over me, and his lips are dry and we spend a few minutes like that, gentle kisses on his dry lips, and then he starts to laugh and I am offended. "Why are you laughing?" I ask, and he laughs more, and I sort of push him and pick up one of the better coats on the bed, with a shiny lined inside of burgundy, and I put it on for a second even though I'm not cold and I ask him again why he laughed and he says, "We went to grade school together," and I say, "We did? We did?" and he tells me his name and then he tells me my name and I apologize because I don't remember him. "I remember you because you were the one with the inheritance," he says, and I tell him I was really good at painting too and he says, "Really? I don't remember that."

So I am through with him.

I take off the coat and throw it back on the bed and then head to the door.

"Wait, why did you kiss me?" he asks, and I know it is taking a big effort for him to string this sentence together because he is so drunk. "Let's go out sometime," he slurs. "I just laughed because it's funny, it's funny. To kiss someone you knew as a kid. It's funny."

I turn around and he looms above me and I can see the freckles on his collarbone and that means he has a chest of freckles and a back of freckles and knees of freckles and freckled inner thighs and I was the best artist in grade school for several years until that dumb girl moved here from Korea, and he is laughing more because he knew me as a little kid and is remembering something and I barely remember what it was like to be a little kid so it seems rude that he would recall something about me that I couldn't myself. If I can't remember it, then it should mean no one else can either.

"No," I tell him. "I don't want to go out with you, ever."

And I'm back in the main room. I return to the same wall. The redhead follows me out and collapses back into that chair, staring, but I ignore him and look at the table of food instead. The guacamole dip is at half, and there are little shit-green blobs on the tablecloth. The brie is a white cave. The wineglasses are empty except for that one undrinkable red spot at the bottom. I go refill my glass and the redhead closes his eyes in the chair. One down.

The blond is next, and he is someone I used to date and in fact only broke up with around three months ago so I think it'll be easy; I find him in the corner talking to two other guys and I glide over and because I am me I am wearing an incredible dress tonight; this one looks almost like it is made of metal; it has this slinky way of falling all over my hips and I feel like an on faucet in it and of course I am the most dressed up at the party, I always am, but that's the whole point, so when the host inevitably looks down at her everybodyownsthemjeans at the front door and says, "Oh, but it's not a formal party," I smile at her with as many teeth as I can fit and wink and say, "That's fine, that's fine, I just felt like wearing this tonight." Inevitably, the next time I see that same host she has more lipstick on or a new glittering necklace her mother bought her but lady she is dust next to me inside this silverness. I am now almost right behind the blond man who broke up with me because he didn't feel loved and it was true, I did not love him, but he is the type to never go out with someone for a long time anyway so we would've broken up soon regardless and I just gave us a good excuse. I am next to him by now and I tell him we need to talk and could we go in the bathroom? He is confused for a minute but then agrees, and says "Hang on" to his friends who shake their heads because they remember me well and think he's being stupid and they're right but we go into the bathroom and I say, "Adam, I have a goal to kiss you tonight," and he says, "C'mon, is that what this is about?" and I tell him to come here but he has his hand on the doorknob but also he's not gone yet. "You're incredible," he says, shaking his head, and I feel mad, what does he mean, it's not a compliment, and he's out the door. And he's out the door, then. I'm alone in the bathroom and I'm sitting on the sink and my butt is falling a little into the sink part, faucet on faucet, and I turn around to myself in the medicine-cabinet mirror and check my teeth and they are bright and white because last week I bought a new tooth cleaner and it's working and my eyeliner isn't smeared because I bought the new eyeliner that swears it won't smear or you can sue the company, and I'm sitting there plotting my next blond when Adam comes back into the bathroom with determination and closes the door firmly. "You're just playing with me, aren't you?" he says, and I say, "Yeah," and he sighs a little. "At least you're honest," he says, and I say, "Thanks, I try to be honest, I do, that is one of my good qualities." He waits there by the door and I hop off the sink to go to him, stand and face him, and he's not running away so I'm moving in and then we're kissing, that easy, and his lips are the same ones I know well, in fact he was my longest boyfriend so I know his lips better than anyone's, and his upper lip is much thinner than his lower lip which I always liked and I kiss that pillow at the bottom and we kiss and it gets more, we keep kissing and I remember just what it's like and I am suddenly feeling like I miss him and I am remembering everything of what it's like to be with him and I am forgiving him for everything and we're still kissing and his teeth and his smell and we've been kissing too long now, it's gone on long enough, so I pull away. He has lipstick on the edges of his mouth. "Okay," I say, "thank you, okay." He looks shook up but also wants more and he has the same feeling I do; he felt the room change into a different room during that kiss but I'm trying to get it back to being the first room, the one where I know it all. His hands are all over my silver dress slip-sliding around and the bathroom door opens, it's some lady who wants to use the bathroom and she sees us and blushes and I'm glad I don't know her because I don't want the whole party to know I'm in the bathroom kissing a blond while I still have a black-haired man to finish the night with. Adam is wiping the lipstick off now and his hand is still on my dress, on my hip; "You're a cold woman," he says to me, and then his hand is gone and he leaves and I am left in there again and I know I am not a cold woman because the whole point of why it was hard for him to leave just then is because I am a not-cold woman but I resent the lie anyway. I check myself in the mirror again and my skin has sharpened and the teeth and eyeliner are all still good and I am thinking about him for a minute, thinking about how when he came inside me and I came outside him he would say something like "This is it," and I'd think, It's the end of the world, and then we'd finish up and be sweating and hot and the world would still be there, like it had swung up and met us. And when we slept then it was so deep it really could've been the end of the world with sirens and megaphones and panicked TV people and I know at least for myself I wouldn't have even noticed.

I exit the bathroom after I've used it and the lady who interrupted is standing there and she is embarrassed and I am not and I step on her foot as I walk out and she says, "Oops, sorry," like all women do and I am mad at that because it was my fault so why is she apologizing? and I hate that she said "Oops" in that little meek voice and now I'm in a bad mood. And I still have one flavor to go. It's an hour later now and the guacamole is gone and the brie is all shell and these stupid people don't know that the white part of brie is important to the taste, that it doesn't count if you only eat the mushy inside, that the French would leave en masse if they came to this party and saw the Americans carving out their cheese like cave dwellers, but the party people only like easy cheese, and easy jeans, and they are all sipping from their fluted glasses and I get refill number three or four and the wine is making my bones loose and it's giving my hair a red sheen and my breasts are blooming and my eyes feel sultry and wise and the dress is water. Adam is back with his friends and he won't look at me and they are sheltering him like a little male righteous wall and the redhead is gone by now or passed out somewhere and I am looking for black hair, looking, looking, and you'd think it'd be easy considering something like four-fifths of the entire earth has black hair and I do find one prospect but he seems harsh and too talkative so I pass him up and I find a cute black guy but he seems to be one of the married ones and I am trying to keep this as simple as possible and I'm looking, still looking, then bingo: it's the tallest man in the room. He has sharp black hair over his ears and glasses and a swarthiness and he is the smarty guy and he is talking to a woman who is clearly entranced by him, but remember: I am a column of mercury, and this woman is wearing a blouse and khaki pants, drinking water from a mug imprinted with water lilies. The deal is done.

She is telling him about her job at a pet hospital. She is a vet of sorts. Every person on earth likes a vet except me, because I think there are too many animals in the first place. And when these vets keep saving the sick animals, we are just stuck with more.

"These are from the last cat," she is saying, holding up her arm which is covered with raised tracks.

He nods, observes. I, however, am not interested in her fake drug habit look-alike war wounds. I bet a thousand dollars she grew up with a dog who had a name with a *y* or an *ie* at the end. I had a dog once, a big dog, a Great Dane, and I named him Off so when I called him, I said "Off!" and he came bounding over. It really fucked with people's heads. At the dog park no one got it. They kept trying to figure out how I did that, if I was okay, what was happening. I was laughing all the time at the dog park. I wore dresses there too and I think people brought their friends to see me, like I was a sight in the city, a tourist attraction. If I was forty it'd be a problem but I'm not so they adore me. Off died early because he was a purebred but I didn't put him to sleep, I kept him company and stroked his big forehead until I saw his eyes shut on their own. I had him cremated. I sprinkled most of his ashes into my plants, but fed a few of the remaining ones to the cat next door because she had always been tormented by Off's size and I thought it was a little bit of sweet vindication.

It's nearly midnight, and I'm waiting for the man here to say something so I can form my game plan. Adam is talking to a woman now and I can tell he is appearing extra animated to get my goat. I can only see the woman's butt from here, but it's very flat and Adam is an ass man so I'm not worried. I don't shrivel up into wiggly jealousy. Instead I feel like thrusting through all the women here, stepping on all those dainty toes, releasing a chorus of "Oops, sorries," a million apologies for something I did wrong.

The vet is still talking. "Last week," she is saying, "the sweetest beagle came in with some kind of dementia and I had to put him to sleep . . ."

"That must be tough," he says, "to put a dog to sleep."

I'm underneath the yellow-and-pink floral painting. Fuck me, I'm thinking. She is taking too damn long. At the door, one of the couples is saying goodbye to the host. Her hand is on his elbow. The host looks dampened; I think somebody broke her stereo.

And suddenly, in a wash, I am feeling low. I am feeling like there is nothing in this whole party for me and I want everyone to leave now. I'm thinking about how when I filled out the evaluation for the painting teacher, and I said she should be fired, I made sure to sign my name. I've given some money to the university–not enough to get a building named after me, but close. And when the next session rolled around and I looked for her name in the catalog, I couldn't find it anywhere. My final painting for the class was that–the catalog page without her name in it.

"Oh," she had said, "isn't that a delightful picture of the sea."

I slump a little on the wall. The red-haired man is back, asleep in his chair. Vet says, "I feel like I'm a prison guard or something with all this lethal-injection stuff."

And then the man says something about how he worked in a prison once and he saw a lethal injection once and it was the worst thing he'd ever seen and I perk up then, rejuvenated, because that's all I need to know; I figure now if he worked in a prison then he has sympathy with people who are trapped or bad and just like that my plan is set.

So I smile at both of them as I move away from the wall in a silvery wave and he notices me then, how can he not, and he nods and khaki vet is off talking again and I interrupt and say, "I have to do something," and the vet is surprised that I can talk and gives me a snotty look down her I-never-got-past-my-childhood-dream nose, and I say, to him only, "Hey, if I'm not back here in a couple minutes, will you check on me?"

He nods, unsure what I mean. She slivers her eyes at me. I open mine wide back, because eye slivering is for old hags. I'm not sure about the details of my plan yet but I step past Adam who is still talking to that unfuckable woman with no ass and I go into the bedroom. I'm planning on stealing something, but I'm not sure what to steal that would make him come find me. I survey the bed. I could steal all the wallets but it seems too unoriginal and detailed so I decide to do the thing I wanted to do with the red-haired man and that is to steal all the coats. I lean over and scoop them together, wool ones and tweed ones and velvet ones and cotton ones, and pick them up in a huge stack, my arms a belt, so heavy they make me stagger, and I go inside the bedroom closet with them and shut the door until I am smothered with coats. It's hot in here, and it smells like shoe polish. I arrange myself underneath the billion coats and then I wait for either the black-haired man to remember to hunt for me or someone else to get ready to leave the party. After just a few minutes, there are footsteps in the bedroom and it's two people and they're ready to bundle up for outdoors and go back to where they live and of course they cannot find their coats and it's winter and they are certain they brought coats. So they leave the room and return to the host and I can hear her quizzical voice going up. "Coats? Bedroom." Her tone is always so sincere. In high school her mother wouldn't let her shop at certain stores because they were too expensive and too slutty and so I would take her shopping and buy her a blue leather miniskirt or a sheer black slip and she would try them on at my house in the ultra-mirrored bathroom and model and pose. She refused to wear them out. She just wore them for me. She has this compact body and looked sporty in everything and I told her compliment after compliment and we never touched but she still always blushed like crazy. There was this one dress of white feathers and she looked like a whole different genre of person inside it. It would've made my entire high school worthwhile if she'd worn that to her prom but she could hardly leave the bathroom and her face was bright red so that between her and the dress I was reminded of a peppermint. I never took those outfits back to the store; I kept them for a few of her visits and when she seemed bored of them or started to guilt-trip me and ask how much they cost, I gave them to Goodwill. Goodwill, for good reason, loved me. And my head is leaning back on a soft coat of lamb's wool and I can hear the talking outside getting louder and I'm thinking that the reason I kept going out with Adam in the first place was because when I showed him my painting of the ocean in my living room, on our second date, when I was wearing peach velvet, long sleeves, super plunging low neck, he looked at it for about one second and said, "Lady, you are screwed UP." And even though I was a little bit insulted, I was also ridiculous with gratitude and I took off my clothes right there, in one smooth movement, unzipped that peach velvet to show a different kind of peach, a different kind of velvet. Within seconds he was kissing my shoulders and my side and the inside of my knee and he told me to stay standing for a while then and I felt like the tallest person ever born. And by now the couple is back in the bedroom and the party is filtering into the bedroom because they know something is wrong and they are all wondering where all the coats are and someone is getting upset, someone with an expensive coat and I reach out my hand and grope around until I find it. Cashmere. It smells like a woman, like expensive perfume, but not as rich as me; me, I buy perfume so expensive it doesn't smell like anything but skin. And they are panicking and someone is saying how the pocket of her coat has her keys in it and she's asking, "Who is missing? Who took the coats?" and I am touching the pocket with the keys, it's near my foot, and I hear Adam call my name and I am quiet but he is thinking, It's her, she is somewhere hiding with coats, and he excuses himself from flat butt but I don't want to see him ever again, I want the black-haired man to find me so I can kiss him and get home already. I close my eyes, hoping that when he opens the closet he will find me sleeping and I'll wake, disoriented; I'll tell him in a delightfully raspy voice that I was cold and needed a blanket and he will think I'm a nut or drunk but also he will be moved somehow and we'll start kissing in the bottom of the closet and he will have intuitive knowledge about my mouth, and I am hearing footsteps approach the closet, heavy ones, male ones, nearby, someone is approaching the closet and it's opening a crack and then it's open but I can't see who's there because my eyes are closed and then it's the black-haired man, it is, I can tell because he says "Oh," and I recognize his deep voice. I reach up a hand because I want to drag him in here—I am stuck, I am bad, it's jail, it's just like you like—but instead, he calls out, "Hey! I Found The Coats!" really loud, and then I pretend to wake up and say "Oh, hi, what? I was just cold," and the host comes by and when she sees me it's like I'm her troublesome dog-pet and she says "I'm so sorry," and the black-haired man points me out and says, "Here You Are, Miss," like he's a bellhop locating luggage and I explain how I was cold and the coat couple reach in the closet as if I'm not even in it and fuss around and retrieve their coats and then they're off and everyone else is taking their coats really fast in case I'm somehow going to eat them and it's a time-limit thing and coat after coat is picked up until I'm coatless and just myself in my dress and I feel truly cold now and bare and small and then Adam is standing there in the crowd, and he says, "I'll take it from here," and I think that's so fatherly of him it makes me feel sort of sick also because it makes me feel sort of good and the host asks what I was doing, and for the third or fourth time I say I was cold, I just thought I'd be warmer with all these coats. I make my eyes blurry. And she buys it. She thinks I'm that plain drunk from her affordable-yet-delicious wine. And the black-haired man buys it too and nods but then turns around and goes back to the other room to talk to the vet. He leaves the drunk crazy lady behind and returns to the conservative animal lover. And it's just Adam there now, standing with his familiar face, who knows I wasn't cold or drunk, standing there as everyone clears out and he tells me to get up and pulls me when I don't and sits me on the bed. We stare at the wall together. And I'm thinking how I didn't reach my goal and that the whole strawberry/vanilla/chocolate trio isn't nearly as good with just two flavors, and he is sitting there thinking something else, I have no idea what, and he isn't touching me but I can hear him breathing. In the other room, people are leaving. The hidden coats scared them and they took it as some kind of cue that the party was over. Everyone is trickling out and thanking the host and whispering about me and she continues to be ultra-sincere, even when some complainer says something about a wrinkle in her coat, in a mad voice. Oops, I think. Sorry. I stare at the wall directly ahead. There's a painting of a desert hung up. It's in a simple wood frame and in it there's just a row of cacti and then the sun setting in the distance and who needs weapons when they're cacti. That's all I'm looking at when Adam takes my hand.

The
Meeting

The woman he met. He met a woman. This woman was the woman he met. She was not the woman he expected to meet or planned to meet or had carved into his head in full dress with a particular nose and eyes and lips and a very particular brain. No, this was a different woman, the one he met. When he met her he could hardly stand her because she did not fit the shape in his brain of the woman he had planned so vigorously and extensively to meet. And the non-fit was uncomfortable and made his brain hurt. Go away, woman, he said, and the woman laughed, which helped for a second. He trailed the woman for a few days saying it was because he had nothing else to do, but in truth he did have plenty to do and he did not know why he was trailing her. His brain made a lot of shouts and static about his brain's own idea of hair color and sense of humor and what animals the woman he met would like (mammals) and his brain's own idea of how to be a member of the world, and everything that was sort of like him and yet different enough and still: this woman he met was the woman he met and however you try, you cannot unmeet.

His brain was in an utter panic at changing. His brain was very pleased with its current shape and did not want to shift, not one bit. This woman liked *reptiles* and *fish*. What sort of decent human being could possibly like reptiles and fish?

He said, Go away, woman. You go away, she said, shooing him with her hand. You're the one following me around all the time.

They went on a walk—or rather she went on a walk and he asked if he could join her—together over the small bridge which ran over a dry stream and looked down at rocks which jutted up like teeth. She talked significantly more than he expected the woman he met to talk and so while she was talking he thought she is surely, and clearly, not the woman for me. Blabbermouth, he thought. She paused at an oak tree and said, Did you stop listening? and so he started listening again and said some stuff himself, about this, about that. He liked talking to her. The woman said she did not know why she liked him, as he was being something of an irritation with all this static in his head and he said he was sorry, he liked her too, but his brain kept rejecting her and he did not know what to do about that. The woman said, Please, would you shut your brain down for five seconds and let the world participate a bit? No, said the man, I control the world. The woman's laughter bounced off the rocks below. The man laughed too but inside he still meant it.

The woman said goodbye and went to her cottage and made some spaghetti and the next day guess who was at her door. Good afternoon. How are you, how are you. The spaghetti was fine-tuned and she was beautiful in the filtered sunlight and they made love that afternoon with the green sunlight through her green curtains. Her body was new to him and he did not like the way her shoulders were so broad and he very much liked the slope of her hips and he was scared because he did not know how to navigate the curves they made together. Later, when he would become a ship's captain on the waves of the water of their bodies, it turned out that those broad shoulders were the thing he would think of with the most lust and the most tenderness. Those broad shoulders would be what he would recognize in a crowd if they all had paper bags on their heads. Those broad shoulders he could spot across an ocean.

The following day, after the green-curtain day, he was back. They ate cold spaghetti out of paper cups on the stoop. He said, I just don't know if I want to marry you. She snorted. What? He said, I'm sorry but I'm just not certain that you are my future wife. She spit some spaghetti out on the stoop in a little red clump and he thought it was gross and she was laughing again, not with, definitely at. He said, I always thought the woman I'd marry would hit me easy, in a bolt of lightning, and there is not lightning there is not even thunder there is not even rain. It all feels, well, foggy, he said. And she said, What makes you so sure I want to marry you? and he said, Oh, hmmm, and she said, Why would I consider marrying a man whose brain is so bossy? I need a man with some *calm*, she said. He looked at her nose, thin and long and her eyes thin and long the other direction and her hair was straight and long and shone. He had a bite of spaghetti off her fork. They sat for a while on the stoop and watched the lizards skit and scat until the mailman came by and delivered some letters—two bills and a postcard from her cousin on an island. She made faces at the bills and laughed at the postcard and scrutinized the little type in the upper left-hand corner telling her where it was and then looked at the picture on the front for longer than he had ever looked at all the postcards of his entire life.

When they made love that day it was one step closer to making sense and she brought them some wine afterward and they sat and watched the sunset through the green curtains, naked, with deep-bellied glasses of wine. The green darkened into black. He let his hand trace each of her vertebrae and she did not say, That tickles, stop, like he thought she might. She just looked out the muted curtain and her hair swished at an angle. He moved his fingers down her whole spine, one by one by one, and during the time it took to do that, his brain remained absolutely quiet.

It is these empty spaces you have to watch out for, as they flood up with feeling before you even realize what's happened; before you find yourself, at the base of her spine, different.

Debbieland

Debbie wore the skirt all the girls had been wearing, but she wore it two months too late. By then the skirt had lost its magic and was just a piece of cloth with some tassels at the bottom. It resembled nothing more than a shred of curtain—something all the mothers had said at the beginning—but for a few months, the skirt had held inside its weave the very shimmer of rightness. If you wore it you were queen of them all, and both girls and boys followed you like strays. But you had to take the risk to wear it even though it was strange, and as soon as enough people caught on, well then. Done with. Back to curtain status. Debbie wore the skirt because she'd seen enough people wear it to know it was okay. She wore the scary skirt safely. For that, we despise Debbie.

We find Debbie in the lunchroom. She is trying, always, to lose weight. We are repulsed by Debbie's cottage cheese and her small styrofoam bowl of pineapple slices. One of us has worn all her rings, in preparation for the harming of Debbie; Debbie, wearing that skirt, eating her pineapple slices by carefully cutting them with the side of her white plastic fork. Soft yellow droplets clinging to her napkin as she wipes her mouth. It is so easy to lure Debbie out. All we have to do is put out some bait, bait in the form of a beautiful magnet that everyone knows, one who sits down out of the blue like a day-dream and asks for a slice of pineapple, please. She shares Debbie's fork. She tells Debbie some casual praise. Perhaps, for the final net, she compliments Debbie on the skirt. Debbie blushes. All day long, she has been in love with her legs swish-ing underneath the skirt, with how the tassels tickle her an-kles. In the corner, our bile multiplies. We feel it passing among us like disease.

The girl who is bait asks Debbie if she will go with her to her car as she has something she picked out for Debbie. Something Debbie might like. It's that easy. The girl who is bait is, today, everything focused on Debbie, and Debbie cannot resist this, could never have resisted it; even when she thinks about it later, there is no twenty-twenty hindsight. It is the stopping of her heart. A dream come true. She has no interest in the boys, or if she does, it is only in how they will make her look to us. And today! The girl has something for her! Something for Debbie! At last it will be true, at last we will have seen Debbie, at last we will have noticed the way she has been improving her walk and clothing choices, and that beauty her one aunt always compliments on the Fourth of July barbecue will finally be a truth in the company at large.

We follow the bait and the fish, hooked. We follow the fate and the wish. Cooked. Silent on our toes. Walk soft, like whispers.

　　We don't wait long. Naturally, there's nothing in the car and only so long that the bait can pretend to rummage around in the backseat. After a minute, we pounce. Two of us hold Debbie down against the passenger door. Two others grab her feet so she can't run or kick. The one with rings strikes Debbie several times—a few times hard in the stomach and one fist in the face so it will show, tomorrow. So she will have to explain. Debbie is screaming and crying. We rip the skirt off with our bare hands and her underwear is almost too much to bear, with that pattern that is the knockoff of the expensive one, and a giant maxi pad weighing down the middle. We rip the skirt into pieces, which is what all the mothers have wanted to do, because it is rags anyway, it is a rag skirt, made of rags. The one with the rings slides her hands down Debbie's arms and the rings she bought at the street fair cut lines into Debbie's skin, where drizzles of blood rise freely to the surface. The bait sits in her car, smoking a cigarette and listening to the radio. It's a giveaway; the tenth caller gets tickets to go to New York City.

We release Debbie once she's bleeding, and she slinks off, sobbing. Trying to pull her shirt down over the whiteness of her ass. Shoulders hunched, hair askew. She will never tell on us. She will never be the rat. She has a tiny part of her, the tiniest part, that still hopes this is part of some cruel initiation or test, and that if she passes it, she will still be included.

We think we could not despise Debbie more. But when we realize this, the loathing is bottomless. Possibly we could bait and hook her every day for a year, preying on that tiny hope until all of Debbie's clothes are in a rag pile and her face is a disaster. If it was not so boring, maybe we would.

We do not speak to our mothers. Long ago we gave up on our mothers. All of us, even though some of us don't have mothers at all. Our mothers died, or our mothers left. Our mothers changed form into a toad. Our mothers became presidents of companies or jumped off of buildings. Our mothers gave up everything for us. One of us has a father who beats the mother. We cheer him on. We like to hold the belt in our spare time and slap it against our palm like we are in a movie, with a cigar, and a damsel in silver tinsel that is ours waits privately on the couch. We go home after the Debbie beating, thrumming from some kind of adrenaline high, and somewhere close by, Debbie checks herself in the mirror. We can sense this. We begin to be concerned she might slightly admire her bruise, so we are hoping the bruise is in an unflattering spot. Since Debbie is not particularly good-looking, the odds are high in our favor. In general, we feel terrific about it all, maybe we even call each other up on the phone to talk, but generally the phone is for people like Debbie. We have better things to do. We realize life is not just a dress rehearsal and if you realize it, you don't need a bumper sticker to remind you. We take off our rings one by one and in the sink we wash them clear of any blood left from Debbie's arm. Her arm hairs were a little too black, frankly. We remember this as we stay up late, watching wrestling on TV because it's so funny. We don't mind being tired in the morning; often, we prefer it.

• • •

Many years later, we make a mistake. We make a grand error. It begins with the girl who comes to ask for directions on our college campus because we look like we always know where we are. In our features, we resemble, somehow, a compass on a neck. We see the girl approach us, with that walk of hers, very quick-paced, and her eyebrows seem funny. We have to look twice. Her eyebrows are straight and black and fierce but underneath the arch we see a garden of tiny weak brown hairs growing out from under the black. She is, apparently, in between eyebrow maintenance. She is one of those girls. We, ourselves, have never once given a shit about our eyebrows, which are fine and prosperous on their own. Still, she asks nicely, so we give her directions, and then we follow her, because there's nothing else to do today and our classes are over. At her location we find we are waiting outside. Strangers float past, in particular that embarrassing person with her cell phone talking so loud. If our cronies were here, we would nudge her into a dark corner, but our cronies have gone off to different settings by now and are extremely poor at writing letters.

Where did Debbie go? Who cares. As soon as Debbie was removed from her skirt, we washed her from our viewpoint. She of course will remember us forever. Such is the deal we make with memory.

After about an hour or so, the one with the eyebrows exits her building, which seems like it might hold within it doctor's appointments. We follow her. Eventually, she looks behind her. We ask her her name. She recognizes us and makes a witty comment. Because it is college, we seem less like a stalker than we will later in life. We are not sure what is going to happen as we are only one today, and therefore less certain, but there is something in those eyebrows that makes us take her hand unexpectedly near the lower parking lot. We end up kissing her by the fountain that is straight shoots of timed water. She is not as surprised as we might expect. She seems to be used to this. We end up kissing her for an hour, and her lips are so soft they are almost like a joke.

It lasts almost a year. It is our longest relationship. She has nightmares all the time, and huddles into our armpit in the darkness, but during the daytime she walks like she's a cartoon hero. We actually catch some of her tears in a vial and hold it in our pocket and finger it when she's at events working the crowd with all her teeth doing all that business. We grip the vial of tears knowing that at any moment we could expose her and the crowd might turn and tear her to pieces. We want to take care of her every minute. We want to make sure her eyebrows are safe; every time she shows up with those weak brown hairs growing in like poor weeds, like murmurs from a third world country, we are filled with a desire to strangle her while we whisper her name for the rest of our lives. We are worried all the time because she seems like the type to walk into danger without realizing it; after all, she let us kiss her by the fountain in broad daylight. She, however, is not worried about herself, or about us. We are very rarely the receptacles of worry, what with that compass we hold upon our neck.

On month eleven, she leaves us. She finds the tear vial creepy, and she's annoyed with the constant worrying and questionings. After waxing her eyebrows until they are invincible, she goes somewhere else, to ask someone new for directions. She has taken on a new map; us, we have lost our sense of order. We find ourselves heading over to sit by the same wall where we met her. We go there every day. We go there too often. We cannot stop going. We end up Debbie.

Many years later from that, we meet Debbie again. It is not at the reunion because we don't attend reunions. We have lost touch with one another anyway, and why else would we go? The rest of the people in high school were an uninteresting blur. We do not know who Debbie is, but she knows who we are, as we sit outside at Bob's Coffee Shop on Wilshire Boulevard pulling change from deep inside our pockets. She has a couple of kids that she is lugging along, and she stops to say hello. Remember? she says. You used to beat me up?

We squint. She is not recognizable; this woman is a middle-aged woman, with her hair cut short for practicality. Do I know you?

She describes the whole incident, and when she mentions the skirt it clicks into place. Oh, we say. Yes. Oh, we are sorry, we say, because at this age it is appropriate to say, even though we do not know if we are sorry. We do not know if we would do it again, if we had the chance, if we were surrounded by our friends and hula-hooping with pineapple rings.

She sits down. The baby on her lap is blue-eyed and has light hairs on its arms, unlike Debbie, with that black hair we still dislike intensely. The older child, also a girl, lolls behind her, looking at the stand-up menu. She is wearing expensive clothes and something about her mouth is very ungrateful.

Why did you do that? Debbie asks simply.

The waiter comes and retrieves our change, annoyed by all the linty pennies. Anything else? he asks dryly. The baby burbles.

We stare at Debbie's baby, who looks like it is from another person's body. Boy? we ask. Girl, she says.

It's Debbie, right? we ask.

No, she says, wincing. My name is Anne.

Oh.

We can't think why we have always been sure she is Debbie. Did she change her name?

I don't know, we say. I don't know why we did it. Sorry? we say again.

She shifts the baby like a sack of flour.

Everyone I tell the story to says you must have been feeling pretty awful about yourself to do such a thing, she says to us, gripping the top of our chair with her hand.

We listen and nod. We realize now that it has been a good story to tell people. She must get a lot of sympathy, and she has always enjoyed sympathy. Suddenly we feel she must owe us a thank-you for giving what would be an otherwise fairly dull life a little bit of texture. She stands and holds the baby close, and the baby starts to cry.

It was a good time, we say. We do not mean it in the shocking way. We just mean it was a good time, then, high school. We appreciated that time.

Debbie leaves. She doesn't say goodbye. She has more fodder for her insulted self; she has a new way to tell her old story. We give up our table which is being eyed by new customers. Cars toil at the stoplight. We glimpsed sympathy for Debbie, yes, when we stood at the wall after our lover left us. We found ourselves hungry and desperate in the pit of the stomach, revolting to ourselves. Then we got over it. We don't go by that wall anymore. Sure, we think of our old gal sometimes but unlike Debbie, we know what should be kept to ourselves, not available for public consumption. Sure, we still keep the tear vial in our car, even though we understand how it could be perceived as creepy. Most of it has evaporated anyway. If we ever happen to see her again, though, we like to think we could prove to her that she cried in our arms, just in case she is pretending to have forgotten. We hear, through college acquaintances, that she married some man. Of course. She always was predictable. We hear she is possibly pregnant. All we know is that her nightmares were intense and we were very comforting then, and we said smart things, and when she was crying in the middle of the night we were paramount, and that sort of connection does not evaporate. We own her, we think, as we walk west down Wilshire, toward the tar. The sky is an easy breezy blue. Perhaps, in a way, we own Debbie too. Perhaps, in a way, if anyone cries on us, we then own them, a piece of them, forever. Perhaps the vial is redundant. It seems nice, to think this. We begin the long walk home feeling refreshed. We look for who we can see crying, because after all, crying is not an endangered action. There are endless tears to hunt down and possess. To provoke or extract or soothe. We are delighted with this new world, this world full of possibility.

Part Two

Motherfucker

The motherfucker arrived at the West Coast from the Midwest. He took a train, and met women of every size and shape in different cities—Tina with the straight-ahead knees in Milwaukee, Annie with the caustic laugh in Chicago, Betsy's lopsided cleavage in Bismark, crazy Heddie in Butte, that lion tamer in Vegas, the smart farm girl from Bakersfield. Finally, he dismounted for good at Union Station in Los Angeles.

"I fuck mothers," he said to anyone who asked him. "And I do it well," he added.

He was also reasonable; he didn't fuck married mothers,

only available ones who wanted to date and who'd lined up an appropriate babysitter for the child that'd made them a mother in the first place.

He wined, dined, danced, romanced–martinis and kisses on the neck, bloody steak and Pinot Noir–the word "beautiful" said sincerely with a casual lean-back into a booth. He asked pointed, particular questions. By midnight had most of them in bed, clothes off in a flash, the speed of a woman undressing changing rapidly over time, faster and faster, and he was a very good lover, attentive and confident, a giver and a taker, and the mothers lined up to see him, their babysitters growing rich, twenties stuffed in those tight teenage pockets.

He never liked any of them for longer than one or two times. Or, he liked them but not enough to keep calling. I love all women, he told himself. He liked to try on hats in stores.

One afternoon, he was at a fancy Bel Air party on a damp lawn talking to some damp-and-fancy people. They stood in groups of three and four, stirring lemonades laced with vodka, that liquid shark swimming among the yellow feathers of their drink. The motherfucker wandered across the lawn to the starlet, famous for her latest few films, wearing the red straw hat and matching red dress, the one watching her four-year-old play on the lawn chairs, the one whose husband had left her for a man, or so said the newspapers. Everyone else was afraid to talk to her.

She had shiny hair under her red hat and was drinking nothing, hands still at her sides.

The motherfucker told her he liked her hat. She said, Thank you. He asked about her son; she said, He's four. The kid rolled in the grass, collecting stains on his clothes like lashings from a green whip.

"I think you're a good actress," the man said. "Why do you always pick such sad characters to play?"

"Me?" she said. "Sad characters?" And she flashed him her teeth, the long white ones that had been photographed a million times by now, each tooth a gleaming door into the mysteries of her mouth.

The motherfucker said yes. "You," he said.

He stood with the starlet for a while and told her he was a graduate student at the school for emotional ventriloquists. She raised one carefully shaped eyebrow. "No," he said, "it's true." She laughed. "No," he said, "it's true. You throw your emotions on other people in the room," he explained, "and see what they do then."

"So what do they do?" she asked, keeping that perfect eyebrow halfway up her forehead.

"It depends," he sighed. "Sometimes they lob them right back at you.

"Turns out life," he said to her, "is a whole lot like tennis."

They walked to the gazebo. The party was ending, and the

sun was going down and the grass had turned a softer shade of green. He knew he needed to do something to make her remember him so he stood there with her in the gazebo, watching her son, and put his hand on her famous shining hair, just for a second, lifted it off her back and let it down again. She jumped.

"Oh!" she said. "Oh," he said, "your hair was stuck."

Then he didn't touch her again, not for weeks.

He got her phone number from the host. Motherfuckers have their ways. It took only one lie and he left with those ten numbers, one dash, and two parentheses tucked with care inside his shirt pocket.

At home, he put in a call to crazy Heddie from Butte. He asked her a half hour of penetrating questions and then tried to have phone sex but found he couldn't really muster up the gusto. His mind was elsewhere. The next day, he called the starlet and asked her to dinner.

She laughed. She sounded even prettier on the phone. "Aren't you afraid of me?" she asked. "After all, I am a movie star." He said no, he wasn't afraid of her, he thought of her as an interesting, attractive woman who happened to have a very public job. She said that was sure a new way to put it. They set a date to meet at an Italian bistro on Vermont, and there she signed twelve autographs and he asked about how what she did as an actress and what he did as an emotional ventriloquist were similar, but she said they were in a restaurant and it was too distracting so they should talk about something light while they were there. "Maybe *you're* afraid of *me*," he said. She looked closer, eyes green and piercing. "Maybe I am," she said, and the rest of the dinner was quiet. The waiter asked for an autograph on a napkin, and by the time they left, it was already hung up by the host's podium with a red thumbtack, next to some signed black-and-white photographs of other stars, many of whom by now were regular people or else dead.

The motherfucker recognized one of the mothers he'd fucked at a table to the right and waved while exiting but the mother didn't acknowledge him because she was jealous and also starlets made her nervous.

The starlet found the motherfucker trustworthy so she invited him back to her new house in the dark curves of the Hollywood hills, the wood floors brown and shining, the pillows sentimental, the magazines unread. They sat and had a good talk on her thousands-of-dollars couch. He mentioned his train trip and she said her father had been a conductor for years. They discussed depots. At the door he did not kiss or hug her but just said he'd had a terrific time, and she closed the door behind him, pensive. She paced a little and then watched some TV. She saw herself on the news.

The motherfucker went home and rented one of her latest movies and watched it closely, and even though it was a comedy, he looked at the smile on her face and decided she was possibly the saddest person he had ever met or pursued.

He didn't touch her even when they went to lunch and she cried about her empty house. About how she had known all along with her husband but never would say it was true to herself. He didn't touch her even when she raised limpid movie eyes up to him and gave him the look that meant Kiss Me to film fans from all over the world. He let his other mothers call and call but he didn't pick up or call back. He invited the starlet to the ballet and during act two, he picked up her hand, and while the stage was full of people as flowers and birds, trying with all available muscles to be lighter than air, their hands learned each other, fingers over fingers, palm on back, palm on palm, edge to wrist, watchbands clinking because both of them liked to know what time it was at all times.

He dropped her off, said he couldn't come in. She was disappointed. She dreamed he was making love to her in a hamper.

Heddie from Butte called. Heddie's father was mad at her about something that had happened four Christmases ago and Heddie was upset. The motherfucker talked to her for a while but he couldn't concentrate and said he had to go write his graduate-school paper on the relationship between sadness, mime, and Ping-Pong. "Why, I didn't know you were in school," said Heddie. "I wish you would talk more about yourself." The motherfucker pretended he had call waiting. His goodbye was rude.

He asked the starlet to dinner again. She was pleased. "He treats me," she told her friend, the other hot new starlet, "like a regular person." "Why on earth," said her friend, the other starlet, "would you want that? What's the point," said the other starlet, "of being a starlet in the first place?" Our starlet put her hand on her cheek. Her blush was the color of a coral reef, but smooth. "I think it has to do with getting emotions thrown on you," she said.

This dinner they shared a bottle of wine and no one stopped to get an autograph. (She was wearing a hat.) She said he could come back to her house again, maybe they could have some tea. They played the hand game under the table and this time the volume was twice as high. His whole body was taut for her. "George is asleep," she said, meaning her son. They drove back and she paid the babysitter, a huge tip to get her out as soon as possible, and she went to the kitchen to put the kettle on, and the moment of the first kiss was prolonged, longer, prolonged; she offered tea, she offered wine, she went to the bathroom and he pictured her in there, looking down at the toilet paper which was not yellow but clear with other liquid, and she returned, sat next to him on the couch, picked up a magazine, stood, sat, stood, sat, and he thought: It has been a while since this woman has been with a man who wants to be with women. And so he just sat there first and thought of women, thought of what he loved about women, thought of the slopes and the jewelry, the lines and the circles, breasts of all sizes, emotion, opening, contraction.

He watched her. She put her head on her own shoulder—coy, twitchy.

"I think about you," he said.

"What do you think about?" she asked. She ran through the movie scenes in her head. They all were very pretty options. He said, "I think about how nervous you are."

Her face fell. "What?"

"No," he said, flustered, "it's great that you're nervous." His expression, for once, was open and earnest. She kept her eyes on him, and laughed once then, the laugh that stole the hearts of a million moviegoers, that fed the wallets of a fat handful of studio executives, and he said, "Wait."

"What?" she said.

He took a step away, and looked at her. She made a wry little joke about directors. Then put her face nearer, ready to kiss him, to prove herself unnervous, how bold, how witty, but he didn't move forward. "Hang on," he said.

She grew bolder, interrupted, said– "Hey. Let's go outside. There are bushes out there." The motherfucker paused and smiled, said no. She twisted and said– "Come with me, let's go to the bathroom counter." She'd had movie sex scenes on the bathroom counter and in the bushes, both. Audiences had liked those a lot. He shook his head, no. "Let's do it on a cliff under a tree!" she sang, and he said no. "I want to make love to you in a bed" is what he said.

This made her feel completely out of control.

He stepped closer. For some reason, his hands were shaking. Using his finger as a pointer, he drew an invisible line around her. He said, "Listen. Look. Desire is a house. Desire needs closed space. Desire runs out of doors or windows, or slats or pinpricks, it can't fit under the sky, too large. Close the doors. Close the windows. As soon as you laugh from nerves or make a joke or say something just to say something or get all involved with the bushes, then you blow open a window in your house of desire and it can't heat up as well. Cold draft comes in."

"It's not a very big house, is it," she said.

"Don't smile," he said. She pulled in her lips.

"Don't smile," he said. "It's not supposed to be big at all. It should be the closest it can to being your actual size."

She could feel it brimming on her lips, that superstar smile, the bow shape, the teeth long and solid tombstones. She knew just what she looked like.

"Don't," the motherfucker said, harder.

And the smile, like a wave at the beach, receded. And when she didn't smile, when the windows stayed shut, the glass bending out to the night but not breaking, the glass curved from the press of release but not breaking, then the tension went somewhere else, something buckled inside her and made the longing bigger, tripled it, heavied it, made it so big the whole house grew thick and murky. This was not something she knew well, this feeling; she was used to seeing her desire like an angora sweater discarded on the other side of the room.

And she felt like she needed him then. In the same basic way she needed other things, like water.

She was up again refilling her cup of tea and he followed her in and as she was pouring it he took the teapot out of her hand and balanced it right on top of the teacup and while she was looking at that, her hands shaking now, he took her fingers and leaned in and kissed her. Took her face in his palms, then suddenly the faces were too close for anything else to be happening and the kiss was soft and so sweet and in the next room the kid shifted and his dream switched to one about lightning and a boy who stuck his hand in the electrical socket and what happened next.

"What do you want?" asked the motherfucker, getting ready to motherfuck, and he stepped into her house and her hands were all over his face, his neck, his bones, his hair.

"Stop asking questions," she said to him, kissing him again. "That breaks open your windows, doesn't it?" And the motherfucker felt he could crush her, because she happened to be right, and he shut up and his house grew smaller, smaller than he was used to, and she didn't smile or run to the bushes, so hers grew smaller, smaller than it had ever been, and then smaller, and then smaller, until she fit inside, gloved, a house of desire the exact size and shape of her. She thought she might wheeze away but then his hands touched skin, and her throat cleared and lifted.

The next morning, a dry clear day, the starlet made the motherfucker banana pancakes. Her son wandered in in pajamas and got some pancakes too. The motherfucker took a shower in her gourmet shower and used shampoo made from the placenta of sea urchin. He came out as fresh and clean as an underwater urchin infant. She was a yield sign, all sinews and mush, and he sat down and she whispered, "That was a wonderful night," and he said, "It was," and he meant it and he meant it too much and he said, "I think I have to go now."

She called him a motherfucker, but in a teasing way.

He said, "It's true, though."

He didn't call her that day. He didn't call her the next day. She realized she did not have his phone number, could not tell him that she had to go on location to shoot the movie about people with problems but would miss him. During her movie the director asked her to smile but she said no. "This movie," she said, "I am going to stay in my house."

On the screen, she was so luminous in her seriousness, she made the whole cinema fill with tension, so much so that every cinemagoer went home charged up like an electrical storm, fingers in sockets, so much so that she got nominated for seven awards. The motherfucker, who never called again, watched her win from the quiet of his small bedroom. She was wearing a dress the color of the sky before it rains and had become, suddenly, beautiful. She had been something else before, but now she was something else from that. She thanked her parents most of all, her father the train conductor, her mother who rode the trains back and forth across the country to be with him. The motherfucker held his own body close. His apartment was very plain. "This is the house of your desire," he whispered to himself, looking at the small walls behind him, and when he closed his eyes, the torrent of longing waiting inside was so thick he thought he might drown in it.

Fruit and Words

So there we were, Steve and I, smack in the middle of the same fight we'd had a million times before, a fight I knew so well I could graph it. We were halfway down the second slope of resignation, the place where we usually went to different rooms and despaired quietly on our own, and right at the moment that I thought, for the first time in seven years, that maybe things were just not going to work out after all, that was the moment he suggested we drive to Vegas right then and tie the knot. "Now?" I said and he nodded, with gravity. "Now." We packed as fast as we could, hoping we could pack faster than those winged feet of doubt, driving 100 miles per hour in silence, from sand to trees to mountains to dry plains to that tall, electric glitter. Parked. Checked in. Changed clothes. Held hands. Together we walked up to the casino chapel but as soon as Steve put his nose in the room, well, that's when those winged feet fluttered to rest on his shoulder. Reeling, he said he had a migraine and needed to lie down. An hour later he told me, washcloth on forehead, that he had to fly home that instant and could I drive back by myself? I stood at the doorway and watched him pack his nicest suit, folding it into corners and angles, his chest and legs and back and butt in squares and triangles, shut and carried.

"Goodbye," we said to each other, and the kiss was an old dead sock.

I spent the day there floating in the glowing blue swimming pool in my brand-new black swimming suit, cocooning myself in a huge white towel that smelled of sunshine, walking past tigers and dolphins. I slept diagonal on the king bed. After checking out, I went to the car, which was boiling hot, and put my bag in the trunk and geared up the engine and turned on the air conditioner and pulled out of the parking structure. The road extended through the desert, a long dry tongue. I didn't feel like listening to music and was speeding along, wondering if to all people the idea of marrying felt so much like being buried alive, as in particular the idea of marrying this man did. Anticipating the talks we were going to have, to get to the point where we both admitted we were only in it out of loyalty and fear, my mouth dried up and I had a sudden and very intense craving for a mango.

I'd never eaten a mango in my life. But the craving was vast, sweeping, feverish.

Great, I thought. It is not mango season and it is not mango country. And I knew those bright flavored gums would not cut it.

After half an hour, the craving was so bad I stopped at a gas station and tried anyway, bought a pack of orange-pink candy–Mango Tango!–but the taste of each flat circle, so sugary and similar to all other sugar flavors, made me long for the real one even more. I stopped at every market I saw but the fruit they had was pathetic: soft mealy apples, gray bananas, the occasional hard green plum.

The road was quiet and empty of cars. I sped past gas stations and fast food.

I was thinking, seriously, of driving straight to the airport and emptying my savings to fly myself to Africa so I could find one there, easy off the tree, the gentle give at the touch of my thumb, when far ahead, several miles up the road, I caught a glimpse of what appeared to be a shack. It was part of a tiny commercial strip facing a doughnut store and an oil lube filter station. From a distance it looked colorful and lively and as I got closer and closer, I thought I might be hallucinating from the heat because as far as I could tell, the front of the shack was full of trays and tables and shelves and piles of ripe beautiful fruit. My mouth started to water and I pulled over and parked my car on the shoulder of the road.

The highway was still empty of cars and the fast food doughnut chain was empty of cars and the oil lube filter was closed, so crossing the street was a breeze. The awning of the store was a sweet blue-and-white gingham and sure enough, there were huge tables burgeoning with fruit: vivid clementines, golden apples, dark plums, swollen peaches, three patterns of yellow and brown pears.

The awning said FRUIT AND WORDS.

I went inside. I found a tan woman behind the counter perched on a stool, dusting a deep red apple with her sleeve.

"Hello," I said. "Wow, you have such beautiful fruit here!"

She had a flat face, so flat I was scared to see her in profile.

"Hello," she said mildly.

My hopes were swelling as I walked by a luscious stack of papayas, surging as I passed a group of star fruit and then, indeed, next to a humble pile of four, I found the small sign that said what I wanted to hear. And there they were, gentle and orange, the smell emanating from their skin, so rich I could pick up a whiff from a distance.

She nodded at me. "They're very good," she said. "Those mangoes are excellent quality."

She placed the polished apple in front of herself like she was teacher and student all at once. I scooped up all four and took them to the counter. I felt a wave of utter unearned competence. Ha ha to everyone else. Finding fresh mangoes fifty miles out of Las Vegas seemed to me, in no uncertain terms, like some kind of miracle.

"You have no idea how wonderful this is," I told her, beaming. "I have been having the most powerful mango craving. And here we are, in the desert of all places!"

She shrugged, agreeable. She'd heard this before.

"Where do you get them?" I asked.

She picked at the point of her eye.

"I get the fruit as a trade," she said. "There's a buyer who likes the salt here so he brings me fruit as payment."

"What a deal for you," I said, "getting all this gorgeous fruit for just a little salt."

I brought a mango up to my nose and smelled the sweetness inside its skin.

The woman sniffed. "It's not regular salt," she said. She indicated behind me with her chin.

"Ah," I said. "What's all that?"

"Those are the words," she said.

I kept my arms full of mangoes and took a step nearer. As

far as I could tell, the entire back wall of the shop was covered, floor to ceiling, with cutout letters. They were piled high on shelves, making big words and small words, crammed close together, letters overlapping.

"Go closer," she said. "You can't see as well from here." She gave me a shove on my shoulder blade.

As I approached, I could see that the words weren't just cut from cardboard. Each word was different. I first saw the word NUT; it was a large capitalized word NUT and it was made out of something beige. I couldn't really tell what it was but then I saw the word GRASS which was woven from tall blades, green and thready, and LEMON, cleverly twisted into cursive with peels and pulp, letting off a wonderful smell, so I went right up to NUT and discovered that it was in fact crumbled pieces of nuts all mixed together into a tan gluey paste.

"Isn't this interesting," I said to the woman.

I found PAPER, cut clean with an X-Acto knife, and a calligraphied ORGANDY, fluffing out so frothy I could hardly read it, and HAIR which was strawberry blond and curled up at the edge of the H and the leg of the R. The man who'd left Las Vegas had strawberry blond hair so I ignored that one and picked up PEARL instead.

"This is pricey, I bet," I said, and she gave me an anxious look, like I was going to drop it. It was stunning, not made of tiny pearls, but somehow of one solid piece of pearl, rippling out rainbow colors across its capitals. I put it back carefully on the shelf next to BARNACLE, prickly and dry looking.

"Why do you make these?" I said. "They're so beautiful!"

And they were. They were beautiful on their own and they were beautiful all together. I thought of her in her desert studio, hands dusty, apron splattered, sweat pouring, hammering down the final O in RADIO. She was making the world simple. She made the world steady somehow.

"People like the words," she told me, picking up her apple to shine some more. "I made them for fun and then I got rich."

"Well, I'd definitely like to buy these four mangoes," I said.

She pressed the register. "Ten dollars."

"And just curiously, how much are the words?" I kept my eyes on that wall, wanting to lean my head on PILLOW.

"Depends," she said. "They vary. Plus, you see, those are just the solids."

"What?" I stroked the petals that made up ROSE.

"I mean those are just the solids. I put the solids on display first because they're easiest to understand."

"Solid colors?" I said, staring at PLAID.

"Solid solids," she said. "Liquids are in the back. Gases are in the back of the back. Both are very pricey," she said, "but I'll charge you just three dollars to look. Three dollars for the tour."

"Liquid words?" I said, and I brought out my wallet. She rang up my mangoes and the tour. I moved closer to the register. "I think I'd like to buy a solid too," I said.

I was feeling, suddenly, more liberated than I had in seven years. I wanted to take over the store. I wanted to bathe in plum juice, rediscover my body and adorn it in kiwi circles. I bit into a mango. The skin broke quick, and the flesh, meaty and wet, slid inside my mouth, the nearly embarrassing free-for-all lusciousness of ripe fruit.

"Oh!" I said. "Incredible!"

She gave me two dollars in change. I licked mango juice off my wrist and turned back to the words.

"Can I buy a solid?" I asked.

She shrugged. "Of course," she said. "Which one?"

I wanted them all so I just pointed to the first I'd seen. "How much for NUT?"

"Interesting choice," she said, walking over and pulling it off the shelf. "NUT. There are seven different kinds of nuts in here. Macademia, peanut, walnut, pecan, cashew, garbanzo, and almond."

I raised my eyebrows, impressed.

"Wow," I said.

She just stood there.

"Isn't garbanzo a bean?" I asked.

She held it out to me. "I'll give it to you for fourteen," she said. "Two dollars a nut."

There was a ten in my wallet between four ones and I lifted them all out. I had another drippy bite of mango.

"I won't eat it," I told her, indicating NUT.

She gave me a lip smile and took my money. "You can eat it," she said. "I don't care."

Scooping all my purchases into a brown bag, she lifted a simple silver key off the wall behind her and beckoned for me to follow. We stopped at a gray door. Before she inserted the key, the woman put a hand on my sleeve.

"Be careful," she said. "These are very delicate words. Don't drip mango on anything."

I had almost finished that first mango by now, the most incredible piece of food I had ever eaten in my life, and I held the remains of the pit away from me. My lips were sticky with juice. I felt the horror of Vegas dissipating, clarity descending like a window wrapped around my heart. She turned the knob, and I followed her in.

The back room was a square with a glass door at the far wall. This room was full of shelves too but the words were even harder to read from far away. I walked quietly up to them.

"Don't touch," she hissed.

The liquid words were set up in two ways. Most of them were shooting through glass pipes that shaped the letters. This looked really neat but I felt a little bit like it was cheating. Some of the others were liquids spilled onto a glass board, forming the letters. This was less cheating but looked cheaper. I walked down the row. I was not thrilled by WATER or COKE. I was drawn to RUBBING ALCOHOL, which was done with the piping and took up almost a whole shelf. It was a good one because it looked just like the water but I trusted that it wasn't. There was one called POISON, no specification, and the liquid was dark brown. The letters were fancy on that one, like an old-fashioned theater brochure. I found BLOOD.

"Real blood?" I whispered, and brought the mango back close to me. Licked its pulpy pit.

She nodded. "Of course."

"From what?" I asked, voice a little higher, and she didn't answer. It shot bright through the pipe as if in a huge loose vein.

I didn't like that blood one. I was recording all of this in a monologue in my head and I wondered then who I would tell the story to, and for the moment I couldn't think of anyone. This made me feel bad, so I went over to LAKE and held that and it had little tiny ferns floating in it and I thought it was pretty. It was next to OCEAN which was looking more or less exactly like LAKE and that's when I wondered if the woman was really truthful and how would anyone know? I wanted to buy OCEAN too, I wanted to have the word OCEAN with me all the time, it was way better than NUT, but I didn't really trust it. It seemed likely that it was, deep down, TAP.

I paused by MILK. The sole white liquid. Soothing, just to look at.

"Gases?" she said.

"Okay," I said. "Sure. I'd like to see the gases, why not."

My hands were now hardening with stickiness, each finger gluing slightly to its neighbor. I wanted to wash them, but instead I dropped the gooey pit into my purse near my wallet. The woman gave me a disapproving look and brought out another silver key, this one from her pocket. She turned and clicked and we went through the glass door in the back of the back room.

The gas room was empty.

"Oh," I said, "hmm." I worried for a second that she'd been robbed and was just now finding out.

"Be very very careful," she whispered then. "This is expensive." She looked tense beneath her tan, each of her features tight in its place.

"More expensive than PEARL?" I said.

"Much more," she said. "This takes very difficult concentration. This is my most challenging work. Look here," she said, "come here and look."

She walked over to one of the shelves on the wall and close up I could see there was more glass tubing—not much, but one word's worth. It spelled SMOKE. Soft granules of ash floated through the M.

"It's a good one," I said. "I like it."

"Most of them," she said, still whispering, "in this room, don't have the tubing."

"Oh." I bobbed my head, not understanding.

"See," she continued, "there are many many gas words in this room but you might not be able to read them."

I looked to the shelves and saw nothing, saw shelves that were empty, saw how my apartment would look in a month when Steve had cleared out his books and his bookends.

"Top shelf: XENON," the woman said. "It's there, it's just very hard to see. I can see it because I have very good eyes for it, because it is my medium."

I looked to the top shelf. "There's no XENON there," I said. "There's nothing."

"Trust me," she said. "There's XENON."

I shook my head. I shifted my feet a few times. There was POISON in the room before, dark and available, and a thin wire of fear started to cut and coil in my stomach.

"ARGON," she said, "is on shelf four, below XENON."

"Noble gas number two," I said.

She nodded. "I prefer the noble gases."

"I bet," I said. "There's no ARGON there," I said.

"It's there," she said. "Be extremely careful."

I spoke slowly, coated now in a very mild shellac of panic. "How," I said, "how can it be there, it would dissipate. I took chemistry. It can't just sit there. Argon," I said, "can't just *sit* there."

"I put guidelines in the air," she said. "I make a formation in the air."

I turned toward the entrance.

"I think it's time for me to go," I said.

"NEON," she said, "is on shelf number three."

But right before I walked to the door, I reached out a hand which was so hard and gluey from the mango juice, reached out just to wipe it slightly on the very tip of the shelf. The coil in my stomach took my fingers there. I barely even noticed what I was doing.

The woman drew in her breath in agony.

"Aaghh!" she choked as I got in my little wipe wipe. "You broke it!"

"I broke what?" I said. "Broke what?"

"You broke AIR," she said. "You need to pay for it, you broke it, you broke AIR."

Then she pointed to a sign I hadn't seen before, tucked half behind a shelf, a half-hidden laminated sign that said: VISITORS MUST PAY FOR BROKEN MERCHANDISE.

"There's air there still," I said, "that's no special air."

"It was air in the shape of AIR," she said. "It took me a while to train that space, it was AIR. That's three hundred dollars."

"What?" I said. "I won't pay that," I said, speaking louder. "I didn't even break it, look, there's tons of air around, there's air everywhere."

I waved my hand in the space, indicating air, and she let out another, louder, shriek.

"That was HOPE," she said, "you just broke HOPE!"

"HOPE?" I said, and now I went straight to the glass door, "Broke hope? Hope is not a gas, you can't form hope!"

The door, thank God, was unlocked, and I swung it open and stalked into the liquid room. The woman was right on my heels.

"I caught hope," she said. "I made it into a gas."

"I want to go now," I said. "There's no possible way to catch hope, please."

My voice was gaining height. I didn't believe her but still. Of all things to wreck.

"Well," she said. "I went to wedding after wedding after wedding in Las Vegas. And I capped the bottle each time right when they said 'I do.'"

This made me laugh for a second but then I had to stop because I thought I might choke. I could just see those couples now, perched at opposite ends of a living-room couch, book-ending the air between them, the thickest, most formed air around, that uncrossable, unbreakable, impossible air, finally signing the papers that would send them to different addresses.

I thought of the seven years I'd spent with Steve, and how at first when we'd kissed his lips had been a boat made of roses and how now they were a freight train of lead.

So that I wouldn't cry, I put my hand near my face and made a pushing motion, moved some wind toward her. "I'm Queen of Hope," I said. "Here. Have some of mine."

She grabbed BLOOD from the liquid room shelves.

"Give me my money for AIR!" she said, waving the BLOOD in my face.

I opened the door to the solid room and ran through it. I kept my back arched so she wouldn't touch me. I couldn't pay the money and I wouldn't pay it, it was air, for God's sake, but I didn't want that blood on me, didn't want that blood anywhere close to me.

"I'm sorry," I yelled as I edged out the front, "sorry!"

I looked past the fruit to locate my car and as I did, my eye grazed over the solid words, familiar now, but on the bottom shelf I suddenly saw CAT and DOG in big brown capitals which I hadn't seen before and my stomach balked. The woman kept yelling "You Owe Me Money!" and I hit the dead warmth of the outside air.

Everything was still. My car sat across the street, waiting for me, placid.

The woman was right behind me, yelling, "You owe me three hundred dollars!" and I took NUT out of my bag and threw it behind me where it broke on the street into a million shavings. "Nut!" I yelled. I got into my car, key shaking.

"Vandal!" she yelled back, and she didn't even try to cross the street but just stood at the front of the blue-awninged store with BLOOD in her arms and then she reached back and pelted my car with a tangelo and a pineapple and one huge hard cantaloupe. I locked my doors and right when I put my key into the ignition, she took BLOOD and threw that too; it hit the car square on the passenger-side window, cracking on the top and opening up like an egg, dripping red down the window until the letters ran clear. Maybe it was just juice, but that one I trusted, that one seemed real to me.

Hands trembling, I put my foot on the accelerator and the car started quickly, warmed from the sunlight, the desert spreading out hot and fruitless. The window to my right was streaking with red now. I kept a hand on the car lock, making sure it was down. Across the street, the woman pulled back her arm, which was an awfully good arm, by the way, she was some kind of baseball superstar, and she let fly a few guavas, which splatted blue against my rear window.

I drove away fast as I could. The shack and the woman, still throwing, grew small in my rearview mirror. I drove and drove for eighty miles without pausing, just getting away, just speeding away as the blood dried on the window, away from the piles of tangerines, from the star fruit clumped in stolen constellations, from the seven different mutations of apple.

In an hour I desperately needed to go to the bathroom, so I pulled into a gas station. I still had the brown bag of mangoes with me. When I opened it up, they were all black and rotten, with flies crawling over them. I dumped the whole bag. The one I'd eaten was just a pit, which I removed from my purse and kept on the passenger seat, but by the time I got home and pulled into the empty driveway, it too had rotted away into a soft, weak ball.

Jinx

Two teenagers were standing on a street corner.

They were both wearing the hot new pants and both had great new butts, discovered on their bodies, a gift from the god of time, boom, a butt. Shiny and nice.

They did not like their butts.

One was complaining to the other that she thought her butt was more heart than bubble and that she wanted bubble and her friend said she thought heart was the best and they stood there on the street corner pressing the little silver nub that changed the mean red hand to the friendly walking man and the light did not change.

One friend had breasts, the other was waiting.

When the light changed, they both walked to the poster store where the cute boy worked. He was growing so fast that he slept fourteen hours a day and when he came to work he had a stooped look like he'd been lifting large objects for hours and in fact there was some truth in that, he'd been un-furling his body up through his spine, up through itself. Each day people looked shorter and today these two girls—the one he liked with the ponytail bobbing, the other one that touched his elbow which he liked too—they were there again looking in the glass case at the skull rings and joking.

The boy showed them a new poster of a rock-and-roll star in a ripped shirt on a stage with a big wide open mouth that you could fall into. The girls, at the same time, said they thought it was gross. Jinx! They laughed endlessly. Too much tonsil, said one, and she grunted in such a way that made them laugh for another ten minutes. It was that fifteen-year-old laugh that is like a stream of bubbles but makes everyone else feel stupid and left out. Which is part of its point. The boy got a break halfway through the time they were there and one girl said she wanted to look at the posters one by one, flipping those big plastic-lined poster holders, because she liked to stare at her own pace, and the other girl, ponytail, went out back with the growing boy, rapidly notching out another vertebra right as they spoke, straightening higher like a snake head rising from an egg. They went out back so he could smoke a cigarette and she smoked it with him and when touchy girl finished flipping through the leather-pants women and the leather-pants men and looked for her friend, she couldn't find her and wandered out of the store by herself.

Ponytail girl leaned over and she and the tall boy kissed and it was carcinogen gums and magical.

She liked to kiss in public, so that if someone had a movie camera she could show people. See.

The other girl, now called Cathy, was on the street alone, looking for her friend who was out back with ash on her lips pushing lips against ash, using her tongue in all the different interesting ways she could think of, her breasts rising.

Cathy, teenager, out on the street alone.

This is so rare. This moment is rare. This teenage girl out on the shopping street alone: rare. She walked by herself, eyes swooping side to side, looking for the bobbing blur of her friend, Tina's, ponytail, but Tina was not to be seen, not even in the dressing room of the cute clothes store next door where they'd recently tried on skirts made of almost plastic that were so short they reminded you of wristbands.

Tina now had his hands on her waist, thinking of that exact skirt right as Cathy walked by it, thinking how it had held in her butt and if she was wearing that plastic skirt now, and he held her butt, it would remind him of a bubble, not a heart.

I do not want guys to feel my butt and think of hearts, she said to herself, that is too weird.

Cathy walked to the corner. She thought, Did Tina leave? She thought she'd head back to the poster store but she sat down on a bench instead and when the bus came she got on. She looked at the people on the bus and no one was looking at her except some creepy old man at the front with those weird deep cuffs on his pants and the seat was cold and Tina was somewhere left out in the stores and would they miss each other? Did she miss Tina? Oh, she thought, probably not. And this was her stop and she got off and walked home, and it was hours too early, they were supposed to be at a movie, and when she went inside her mother was sitting there on the couch looking at the backyard. It was like the whole afternoon had got a haircut that was too short. She sat with her mom, making sure the backyard stayed put, which it did, and when her mom fell asleep it all seemed disgusting and this was what happened in the afternoon and she went and looked at herself in the mirror for an hour and felt terrible even though she liked the pose of her left profile best.

And Tina, done with kissing, done with skull rings–the boy settled back behind the counter after waiting two minutes, counting, to tame his erection–Tina was walking the streets and asking people if they'd seen a girl with a great yellow shirt on. No one had, they thought she meant some older woman but Tina said, No no, and she started to cry on the street because she thought the worst thing, but when she called on the phone just to see, just in case, the most familiar numbers in the world, Cathy answered. Hello? Tina forgot how to talk for a second, she was so surprised, and then she just said, Oh. Oh? Hi. Cathy? Tina? Hi? The two girls bumped around the conversation for a few minutes, but for the first time in life, they didn't know what to say to each other. After a while they just said goodbye and hung up. From then on at school they tended to be friendly but distant and found other people to sit with at lunch. By graduation day, three years later, they had forgotten each other's phone numbers completely, even though they hugged in their caps and gowns and tassels for old times' sake and said, Good luck, Keep in touch, Have a hot summer, Later.

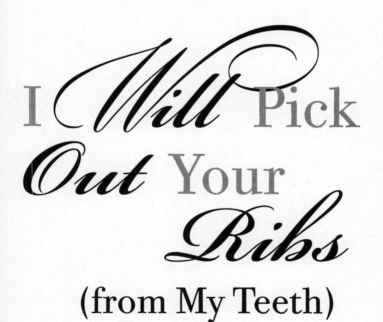

I Will Pick
Out Your
Ribs
(from My Teeth)

Here is my opinion of the emergency room: it's bad.

Here's the deal: everyone is sick and coughing or has some finger falling off or is bleeding all over several Kleenexes or crying because the one they love is taken away to be fixed or not fixed or else running to the bathroom with a bladder infection. I do not think it is a good TV show. I think it is a bad place to be and I go there all too much because I am in love with someone who is in love with hurting herself so the emergency room is our second home.

The nurse knows my name. Sometimes I use a fake name just for fun but she raises her eyebrows and corrects me.

Okay, this seems unrelated but it's not: at Thanksgiving I broke a plate and my mom did not get angry. It was an especially big plate, and after I broke mine there was only one left. "These," she said to me, "have never fit inside the dishwasher anyway and they always break and sprinkle plate dust everywhere." She looked at me. "So," she said, "let's break this last one too."

We went outside and she held it up and then just let it drop. I kind of wanted her to throw it but she had her own style and that's okay. It still broke off into little plate pieces that I offered to clean up and while she went back to the turkey I swept up the pieces and thought about my mother who was not afraid.

But my girlfriend is. Afraid. Of. Name it. I am going to refuse to go to the emergency room after a while but I know I'm lying when I say that. Some things you know you will never stop, your whole life. Some things just stay and stay.

So let me tell you more facts then.

In the emergency room the carpet is yellow and filled with little drops of red (now brown) that you know have been there for years and the carpet cleaning bill should be huge but they just let it go. There will always be more blood, they figure, so why clean up the old stuff? Smarter emergency rooms use linoleum. But my girlfriend isn't a bleeder; she takes pills. I rush her in with her slurry speech and shaking limbs and sometimes I want to take her out of the car and just leave her at the emergency room gutter. I figure they'll find her, but what if they didn't? I saw a dog washed up on the beach the other day and no one saved it. Cute as it was, it was not cute enough. I thought about lifting up the collar and memorizing the number and calling the owner but I couldn't touch its wrinkly neck. I'm not as brave as my mother. She's the one who broke the plate.

My friends tell me I'm an idiot; well, I say, no. They say she'll never die and I'll do this forever and I think they're right but I still can't stop driving that familiar ride to the hospital with the weird three-way stop that takes too long. I tell my friends that I like that emergency room nurse. That it's all a big scam to fuck the emergency room nurse. With her white shoes and bouncy tits and thin knee-highs and my tongue up her dress.

You know the truth: the nurse is in fact old and tired and gives me looks like *I'm* causing the overdoses, right. Me, the nicest person on the face of the earth. Like *I'm* the problem as I sit there and read the same magazines over and over. When I look for the crossword puzzles, they're filled in, and worse: they're filled in by me. And I can't even correct myself because I still don't know the same answers I didn't know last time I was here.

My girlfriend comes out from the back this time with that tag on her wrist and she crawls in my lap and kisses my neck and I grumble to the air.

She's telling me a secret.

We all know what it is.

"Never again," she whispers to me. She thinks I'm so dumb. Like it would even matter. "This is the last and final time."

On the way out the door she wants a candy bar but has no money so we go into the lobby shop and I get her a Snickers and I get myself a coffee and we walk arm in arm to the car. At the car door I find I don't have my keys.

"Wait." I keep checking my pockets, one two in the back, one two in the front, top of shirt. No jingling.

"I'll go get them," she says, "they must've fallen out while you were sitting."

She's so helpful now. Her skin is very pale; she looks diluted. I sip my coffee.

"I'll look," I say, "you stay here."

I race back and the nurse's eyes widen or at least I think they do and my keys are sandwiched in the pages of a magazine causing a pregnant lump and I'm back at the car and Janie is gone. Am I really surprised? She does this all the time. And like usual, there's a little note in my windshield: Took A Walk. See You At Home. Plus a little heart shape. J.

I'm supposed to be mad again. Instead I am interested in

the traffic laws. Car on the right: go. Yellow means slow down. Use your blinker.

I use my blinker. I find myself using it to go into the left left lane and getting on the freeway. This is not where I live. But I love those green signs. I love that they picked green instead of black.

I drive to my friend Alan's house. He answers the door in a towel. I think he's been having sex with his new girlfriend, Frieda from Germany, who he says is the hottest ever. She is walking around the living room naked and her breasts are different, un-American. Oblong. She waves at me. I wonder, Why did he answer the door?

"Just stopped by to say hi," I say. "I was going to bring you that book but I forgot."

"Lunch?" he says.

"Sure." I go into the kitchen and Frieda spoons cereal into a bowl without milk and then leaves again. I can hear her crunching in the living room. Alan gives me a cold barbecued rib and some pear slices and a piece of paper towel and a glass of milk.

"Wow," I say. "It's the perfect lunch."

He leans closer to me. The only reason he let me in is because he wants to talk about her.

"It's so good," he says, rolling his eyes, gripping the table, "I mean: fuck. I mean: go to fucking Germany *now* and get yourself a girlfriend."

I'm gnawing on the rib and loving how it sticks in my teeth.

"Maybe it's not Germany," I say. "Maybe it's just her."

He nods and grips the table harder. "Then," he says, grinning, "you are fucking out of luck."

The skin of the pear is abrasive and rubs the rib juice off my lips.

"Janie?"

"Still alive," I say, "just got back."

"Pills?" He looks away.

"Yup," I say, "same darn pills."

"And you?" He leans back now. He is a decent guy.

"No pills for me."

"No, I mean how are you holding up." He takes a sip of my milk; it's a big sip and it sort of makes me twitch because I was saving it for last. Even though it is rightfully his. Still. I like milk.

"Like I said: no pills." I drink the milk until only one very slow drop is climbing up the side of the glass. I consider how I will back out of his tricky driveway. Make a perfect S shape, with one arm across the back of the front seat, like the seat is my girlfriend. A careful release on the brake while he goes to Frieda and kneels between her legs and the crunching gets louder and louder.

Back home, Janie is in front of the television. It's not on, but she's looking at her reflection in the greenish glass. She doesn't ask me where I was. She's not too good at noticing things like that, like the fact that it took me an hour and a half to get home.

I go into the bathroom and get dental floss. There are rib twigs between all my teeth. How I love to pop them out. One goes flying into the carpet.

"Do you hate me?" she asks. She has her legs tucked underneath her and her head against a pillow and I can see the line of her thigh all the way up. I still think she is beautiful. She won a beauty contest when she was six.

"Nope." I keep flossing.

"Come here," she says, and I go lie down next to her and keep flossing.

"Stop," she says, laying her head on my chest. "I can hear you doing that."

"No," I tell her, not touching her yet; I won't touch her yet.

She presses her face down hard. I stroke her head with my available elbow and her hair is shining like gold in the sunlight through the unopened window. It all makes me very sleepy.

"The thing is," she says, voice muffled out through my T-shirt, "what I said before, you know, never again, I can't really promise that."

"I know," I say.

"I don't really know what will happen."

"I know." I wrap the floss around my index finger like a

ring and watch the blood shift. The tip of my finger turns waxy and purple.

"What would I do without you?" she says, and I get the floss around my wrist this time.

"Same thing," I say as my hand darkens.

When I go to bed I think of Frieda but after a while I get bored. I don't know what Frieda's like. Janie, who I do know, is asleep. All her pill bottles are locked up in the trunk, and I own the key. It'll take her a while this time to find where I hid the key; I'm getting better and better at stumping her. Last month it was floating in the bag of walnuts, and it would've taken a long time for her to find it except I forgot that she loves walnuts. Now we both hate them; Janie because of the taste in her mouth, me because when I found her, they were scattered all over the floor surrounding her and for a second I actually thought they were tiny shriveled lungs with all the air sucked out of them.

This time, the key is hidden under the bathroom counter. Where the lip of the counter rises above the floor? I have taped it. You only notice if you're lying flat down on the bathroom rug, relaxing, or if you're running your hand along the rim. So this round should take at least a few months. One of these days, I'll just do my duty and make a scene and dump all the pills down the toilet like I'm supposed to and Janie will cry and cry and then find herself a new boyfriend.

Until then, it's our best time together. She plays with my hair. She sits on the sofa in the slanted light with her guitar and sings songs with my name in them that she makes up on the spot. When she was six, she won that beauty contest talent competition by singing "These Boots Are Made for Walking" with a pretend guitar slung around her shoulder and a dance routine. All the adults cheered as she stomped about in her country-western outfit. All the other kids started crying backstage when they heard the thunderous applause. We still have the trophy; it's locked inside the trunk with the pills tucked inside the cup part like a sordid story in a celebrity magazine at the airport. The boots she wore are in there too; they're really little, made of thin yellow leather with fringe on top and a silver badge on the side. I didn't have anything special to add, but just to be fair, I put my report cards from junior high school in the trunk too. I got all As. I have always been a good student.

Ironhead

The pumpkinhead couple got married. They had been dating for many years and by now she was impatient. "I'm getting cooked," she told him, and she took his hand up her neck to the inside of her head so he could feel the warmth of the flesh there, how it was growing soft and meaty with time; he reeled from both burden and arousal. Taking her hand, they walked over to the big soft bed and while he unbuttoned her dress, he thought about what she was asking for and thought it was something he could give her. He slipped his belt out of the loops and the waist of his pants sighed and fell open. When the pumpkinheads had sex, it was at a slight angle so that their heads would not bump.

They had a big wedding with a live jazz band, and she gave birth to two children in the span of four years, each with its own small pumpkinhead, a luminous moon of pumpkin, one more yellowish, one a deep dark orange. The pumpkinhead mother became pregnant with her third child in the seventh year, and walked around the house rubbing her belly, particularly the part that bulged more than the rest. At the hospital, on birth day, the nurses swaddled the baby in a blanket and presented him to her proudly, but she drew in her breath so fast that the pumpkinhead father, in the waiting room watching basketball, heard through the door. "What is it?" he said, peeking in.

She raised her elbow which cradled the blanket. The third child's head was made of an iron.

It was a silver model with a black plastic handle and when he cried, as he was crying right now, steam sifted up from his shoulders in measured puffs. His head was larger than the average iron and pointed at the tip.

The father stood by his wife and the mother adjusted the point so that it did not poke her breast.

"Hello there, little ironhead," she said.

The siblings came running in from the waiting room, following their father, and one burst out laughing and one had nightmares for the rest of her childhood.

The ironhead turned out to be a very gentle boy. He played quietly on his own in the daytime with clay and dirt, and contrary to expectations, he preferred wearing ragged messy clothes with wrinkles. His mother tried once to smooth down his outfits with her own, separated iron, but when the child saw what was his head, standing by itself, with steam exhaling from the flat silver base just like his breath, he shrieked a tinny scream and matching steam streamed from his chin as it did when he was particularly upset. The pumpkinhead mother quickly put the iron away; she understood; she imagined it was much the way she felt when one of her humanhead friends offered her a piece of seasonal pie on Thanksgiving.

"Next year," she told her husband that November, "I am going to host Thanksgiving myself and instead of a turkey I'm serving a big human butt."

Her husband was removing his socks one by one, sitting on the edge of the bed, rolling them into a ball.

"And for dessert," continued his wife, stretching out on the comforter, "we will have cheesecake from brains and of course ladyfingers and–" She started laughing then at herself, uproariously; she had a great loud laugh.

Once undressed, her husband lay his head flat on her

stomach and she held the wideness of his skull in her hands and smoothed the individual orange panels.

"I think our son is lonely," she said.

They made love on the bed, in a quiet relaxed tangle, then threw on bathrobes and went to check on their children. The two girl pumpkinheads were asleep, one making gurgling dream noises, the other twitching. They shook the second gently until her nightmare switched tracks and she calmed. Shutting the door quietly behind them, the parents held hands in the peace of the hallway, but when they stepped into the ironhead's room, they found him wide awake, smoothing his pillowcase with his jaw.

"Can't you sleep, honey?" asked his mother. He shook his head. He had no eyes to look into, but the loll of his neck and the throw of his small body let them know he was upset. They sat beside him and told a story about zebras and licorice. He tucked his head agreeably on the pillow and listened the whole time, but his parents tired before he did and tiptoed out of the room, figuring he was asleep. No. He never slept, not because he didn't want to but simply because he couldn't, he didn't know how. He spent a few more hours staring at the wall, feeling the sharp metal of his nose, breathing out clouds into the cramped sky of his bedroom. Around three in the morning, he read a picture book. At five, he snuck to the kitchen and had a snack of milk and cookies. He felt very very tired for four years old.

• • •

At school, the ironhead made no friends because he was expected to be a tough guy due to the sharpness of that metal point, but he was no tough guy and preferred the sandbox to the grass field. He filled buckets with sand and then submerged them in sand. One afternoon, tired of being teased by the seas of children with human heads and his sisters who escaped ridicule by being the best at every sport, he left the playground by himself and went for a walk. He walked past the residential area of town, with the friendly rickety houses and their green-yellow lawns and an occasional free-standing mailbox in the shape of a cow or a horse. He walked past the milkman, whose arms were full with glass bottles of frothy white, all set to be delivered, and who laughed at the ironhead, which just made steam rise from the boy's neck. He walked until he reached a big field, one he'd never seen before. Beyond it was a building. Glancing around, the ironhead crossed the field, lifting his little legs high to clear the tall patches of weeds, and the air was shifting smell now, it smelled bigger than the town did, pollen riding on wide open space, immigrant seedlings.

When he reached the building he saw that it was an appliance shop. COME ON IN! it said on a sign in the window, so he reached high and opened the glass door and entered. This wasn't a large store, but it was the largest he had ever seen, bright white with fluorescent light like the inside of a tooth. He walked down the four aisles slowly, hands in his pockets, passing blenders and sewing machines and vacuums and toasters. Finally he came across the assortment of irons in the middle of aisle three, and here he stopped. There were four or five different styles, some in boxes with photos on them, some freestanding, chin up. He settled himself down across from the irons and looked up at them. He imagined it was a family reunion. Hello, everybody. Nice to see you. He greeted his aunt, his uncle, his cousins. Reaching out, he took the boxes from the shelves one by one and set them in a semicircle around him. They were silent and price tagged and cold company. The ironhead sat there all day long, from ten in the morning to four in the afternoon, breathing a slow hush of steam, and no one in the store even talked to him. Finally the cashier's boss entered, and when he found out how long the ironhead had been there, he called the police. "This is not a public park," he said. "We are trying, after all, to make some money here." In ten minutes, the cop car pulled up, and the two policemen walked over to the ironhead sitting quietly in aisle three trying to take that ever-elusive nap. One cop laughed out loud and the other pretended to pull out his gun in fake terror. "You never know what you're going to see in this podunk town," the laughing one said. "Got any wrinkles on your shirt there, mac?" His partner smirked. The ironhead leaned down and put his head on the white tile so that the boxes of irons rose over him like buildings.

The cashier, who was not unkind, put in a call to the iron-head's worried parents; they drove right on over, hurried in, hugged their son close. One of the policemen cracked a Halloween joke which made the mother livid but she was more concerned when she saw the half-moon of irons around her son's head; she asked him what it meant on the drive home but he just shook his head, snuggling against her warm hip. That night, he lay in bed awake again, for the thousandth night of insomnia, listening to the sounds of his sisters and parents sleeping in the next rooms, which was the most lonesome sound in the world, and by morning was so exhausted, down to the root of his bone, that he begged to stay home from school. Because she loved him dearly, almost more so because he had been a complete and utter surprise, his mother gave him a good lunch of hot dogs and potato chips and chili and milk, set him in front of the TV with a blanket, and left for work herself.

When she came home at five, her ironhead was dead. He was in front of the TV with his ironhead turned toward the sofa, away from the screen, and when he didn't respond to her inquiries, she went to check on him, listening for his breath in its small steamy gasps, and she heard nothing coming out of him at all. She was so used to the slow steady hushed sound of his breathing that it was only the abrupt silence of him that convinced her he wasn't there anymore. She crumpled by his side and held him close and cried and cried and when the little girls came home from soccer practice they didn't know what to do and couldn't stand to watch their mother crying like that and so they got mad at each other and screamed and kicked on the front lawn. The mother held her little ironhead close and his body felt cool and distant. She stroked down the plastic handle and when her husband came home she nearly fell against him.

The doctor who came by that night to state the cause of death said that the ironhead had died of utter exhaustion, that it had nothing to do with the chili or the journey across the field or the iron in boxes or the laughing policemen. He weighed the iron and said that the weight of it was completely out of proportion with the rest of the body, and that it was frankly incredible that the boy had lived at all, carrying a head like that around all day. "This is rock-solid iron, and you can imagine–" he declared. The mother stood still as a stone; the father nodded slowly. The doctor didn't finish his sentence, and bowed his head in the face of their grief. The pumpkinhead family buried the ironhead in the cemetery which was only a few blocks away, and at the funeral, children from the school filled buckets with dirt and then submerged them in dirt. A few well-meaning but thoughtless types brought irons to put on his grave, but the mother, her body taut and loosening at the same time, flung them as far away as she could, flying irons, until they crashed among the trees, shading boat-shaped imprints into the earth. One thrifty mourner secretly collected them and took them with her and sold them for half price back to the appliance shop where they crowded the aisle, chins up. The pumpkinhead family sat together at the cemetery and the mother kept uncovering dishes of warm food so she could release steam on his grave, because she wanted to give him voice, to give him breath again.

For many weeks, all they ate were the casseroles brought by the neighbors. When they ran out of those, the mother went into the kitchen, gathered ingredients, and made spaghetti. She was slow and heavied, but she did it, and the family ate together that night: four. While she cut the mushrooms, she cried more than she had at the grave, the most so far, because she found the saddest thing of all to be the simple truth of her capacity to move on.

Thirty years later when the girls were having their own children, they had mostly pumpkinheads, but the recessive gene did rear its head once more and the second daughter's third child emerged with the head of a teapot. This seemed less difficult to live with than a pointy heavy head of iron and the teapothead child did just fine, made many friends, and slept without trouble. She breathed steam just like her uncle had, and so they sometimes called her ironhead as a pet name even though it didn't fit. She was very good at soccer. The mother and father pumpkinhead still visited the cemetery regularly and sat there with their backs against the dates of their child's birth and death and the mother said, "I can feel my head softening," and the father said, "My shoulders are shrinking and my knuckles are growing," and they sat with their heads orange globes against the gray stone and green grass and after a few hours walked home together.

Part Three

Job's
Jobs

God put a gun to the writer's head.

I'm making a rule, said God. You can't write another word or I'll shoot you. Agreed? God had an East Coast accent, tough like a mobster, but his lined face was frail and ethereal.

The writer agreed. He had a wife and family. He was sad because he loved words as much as he loved people, because words were the way he said what he wanted about people, but this was God and God was the real deal, and he didn't want to spend too much time dwelling on it. So he packed up his typewriter and paper and tucked them in the hall closet, and within two days, to comfort his loss, went to the art supply store and bought oil paints and a canvas and a palette and set up in the garage among the old clothes and broken appliances. He'd always liked painting. He thought he had a good sense of color. He painted every morning for hours, until he started to paint something real.

He was working on his eighteenth canvas, blues and browns in sharp rows blurring in the middle, making a confrontation with black, when God entered his studio, this time holding a dagger.

Cut the painting too, said God. No words, no images. Or– He made a slicing motion near his stringy throat.

Why? cried the painter, already missing the sharp smell of the oils, how the colors mixed to become brand new again, an exotic blush of yellow, a bluish gray, a new way to show trees, with white! He missed the slow time he took washing his hands with turpentine, the way his wife praised the new rugged scent of him.

God lifted the dagger to the lightbulb of the garage and it glinted, unpolished silver, speckled with brown. Do not question God, said God.

So the painter packed away his paints, inside that hall closet, next to the typewriter and reams of white paper. He felt a deep pang, but within a week signed up for a drama class, held in a church where the ceilings were high, the air cool, and every scene took on particular gravity with those stained-glass windows acting as set. He played a few roles, and he wasn't very good at first but was enjoying it anyway, shy man that he was, liking the way he would feel his feeling and then use it and look around at the other people in the class, faces split into red-and-yellow triangles from the windows, and see they were feeling the same feeling with him, how contagious it all was. He needed a lot of reassurance as an actor but he was starting to understand its ultimate camaraderie and loneliness, the connection which is tight as laces then broken quick as the curtain's fall.

So of course one afternoon, walking out of the church, spanking a new script against his knee, he found God in the backseat of his car, gripping a bayonnet.

No more, God said. In my house no less, said God.

The actor started to cry. I love acting, he said. I'm just getting it right, he said. My wife thinks I'm coming out of my shell.

God shook his head.

Mime? the man pleaded.

God poked the actor's side with the sweet triángular tip of the bayonnet.

The actor sat in the car, gripping the steering wheel, already missing the applause, the sight of the woman in the front row with tears in her eyes that were from the same pool of tears he'd visited to do the scene, the entire town fetching water from the same well.

The actor was depressed for a while which his wife didn't like much, but finally he slogged himself out of it and took up cooking. He studied the basics in the cookbook and told himself that patience was a virtue and would be put to good use here. Sure enough, in three months, he'd made his first soup from scratch—potato leek nutmeg—and it was very good. His wife loved it. You're amazing, she told him in bed, his hands smelling of chicken guts; I married the most amazingly artistic man, she said.

He kissed her. He'd made a dessert too and brought it into bed—a chocolate torte with peanut butter frosting. He kissed her again. After two bites the torte fell, unnoticed, to the floor.

God was apparently busy, he took longer this time, but showed up after a big dinner party where the chef served leg of lamb with rosemary on a bed of wild rice with lemongrass chutney. It was a huge hit, and everyone left, drunk, gorgeous with flush, blessed. The chef's wife went to the bathroom and guess who sauntered through the screen door, swinging a noose.

No! moaned the chef, washing a dish. No!

This is it, said God. Stop making beautiful food. What is with you?

The chef hung his head. Then hung up his spoons in the

cupboard with the typewriter, paints, playbooks and wigs. With the pens, turpentine, and volumes of Shakespeare. The shelf was getting crowded so he had to shove some towels aside to make room. He spent the week eating food raw from the refrigerator, and somehow found the will to dial up a piano teacher. But right when he glimpsed the way a chord works, how it fits inside itself, the most intricate and simple puzzle, when he heard how a fourth made him weep and a fifth made him soar, the cheerleading of C major, the birch trees of D minor, God returned with a baseball bat tucked into his belt.

Don't even think about it, barked God.

Dance? Rifle.

Architecture? Grenade.

The man took a year off of life. He learned accounting. He was certain this would be no problem, but after a few weeks the way the numbers made truths about people's lives was interesting to him; he tried law but kept beginning a duet with the jury; chemistry was one wonder after another; even the stock market reminded him of a wriggling animal, and so of course, the usual: pins near the eyes, the closing of the job doors, the removal of the name plaque, the repeated signing of the quitting papers.

So the man sat in a chair. God had ordered him to stop talking, so he went to a park and just looked at people. A young woman was writing in a blank book under a tree; she was writing and writing, and he caught her eye and sent her waves of company and she kept his gaze and wrote more, looked up again, wrote more, circled his bench and sat down and when she asked him questions he said nothing but just looked at her more, and she stood and went away, got a drink at the water fountain, circled back. After an hour of this, she nodded to him, said Thank You, and left. The pathway of her feet looped to the bench and back and away and back, in swirls and lines.

Shut your eyes! yelled God.

The man's wife was unhappy. She was doing all the cooking now and her husband didn't move or speak anymore. She missed their discussions, his paintings, his stories, his pliés. She missed talking to him about her job with the troubled people, and how at certain moments there was an understanding held between her and the person, sitting there, crying or not crying, mad or not mad, happy or unhappy, bland or lively, and it was like, at that moment, she said, they were stepping all over a canvas together. It's like, she said, the room is full of invisible beetles. Or faucets. Or pillows. Or concrete. She told him all about it and his eyes were closed but she could feel, from his skin, that he was listening. She went to him and undressed him slowly and they made love there on the sofa, and he hardly moved but just pressed his warmth to her, his body into hers, and she held him close and the man gave her all he could without speaking, without barely shifting, lips and hips, and she started to cry.

Afterward she pressed her head to his chest and told him all the things she had thought about, the particular flower he made her feel, the blade, the chocolate torte.

They slept on the sofa together.

God put the man in a box with no doors or windows. He tied his hands behind his back and knotted a blindfold over his eyes. He stuck duct tape over his lips. God said: Not a peep out of you. Don't you interact with anybody. The man sat with his head full of dreams. He thought of flying fish and the smell of his wife's skin: white powder and clear sweat. He thought of basil breaking open and the drawing of a tomato with red and black paint and the word tomato, consonant vowel, consonant vowel, consonant vowel, and the perfect taste of tomato with basil, and the rounded curve of a man's back, buttons of spine visible. He wondered where the girl with the half-blank book was right then. He thought of his wife making bridges of air over air. He listened to the sound of wind outside the box, loud and steady as his breath.

Dearth

The next thing in the morning was the cast-iron pot full of potatoes. She had not ordered them and did not remember buying potatoes at the grocery store. She was not one to bake a potato. Someone must have come in and delivered them by accident. Once she'd woken to meadows full of sunflower bouquets all over her house in glass vases and they turned out to be for the woman next door. Perhaps the woman next door had a new suitor now, one who found something romantic in root vegetables.

Our woman checked through her small house but it was

empty as ever. She asked her neighbor, the one whose windows were still crowded with flowers, but the neighbor wiped her hands on a red-checkered cloth and said no, they were not for her, and she had not ordered any potatoes from the store either, as she grew her own.

Back at the house, the potatoes smelled normal and looked normal but our woman did not want them around so she threw them in the trash and went about the rest of her day. She swept and squared and pulled weeds from her garden. She walked to the grocery store and bought milk. She was a quiet person, and spoke very few words throughout the afternoon: Thank You, Goodbye, Excuse Me.

The next morning, when she woke up, the potatoes were back. Nestled, a pile of seven, in the cast-iron pot on the stove. She checked her trash and it looked as it had before, with a folded milk carton and some envelopes. Just no potatoes. She picked up all seven again, and took them across the road and pushed them one at a time into the trash Dumpster, listening as they thumped at the bottom of the bin.

During the afternoon she walked past rows of abandoned cabins to her lover's house. He was in his bedroom, asleep. She crawled into the bed with him and pushed her body against his until he woke up, groggy, and made love to her. She stared at the wall as the craving built bricks inside her stomach, and then she burst onto him like a brief rain in drought season. Afterward, she walked home, and he got ready for his night job of loading supplies into trucks and out of trucks. She stopped by the cemetery on the way home to visit her mother, her father, her brother. Hello mother, hello father, hello brother. Goodbye now.

The next morning, the potatoes had returned. This time she recognized them by the placement of knots and eyes, and she could see they were not seven new potatoes, but the same seven she had, just the day before, thumped into the Dumpster. The same seven she had, just the day before that, thrown into the small garbage of her home. They looked a little smug. She tied them tight in a plastic bag and dropped them next door on the sunflower woman's front stoop. Then she repotted her plants. For the rest of the day, she forgot all about them, but the next morning, the first thing she checked was that cast-iron pot. And what do you know. And on this day they seemed to be growing slightly, curving inward like big gray beans.

They were bothering her now. Even though she was minutely pleased that they had picked her over the sunflower neighbor, still.

"All right." She spoke into the pot. "Fine."

Oven.

On.

Since she did not enjoy the taste of baked potatoes, when

they were done she took them into the road and placed all seven crispy purses in a line down the middle. The summer sun was white and hot. At around three, when the few cars and trucks and bicycles came rolling through town, she swayed and hummed at the soft sound of impact, and that night, she slept so hard that she lost her own balance and didn't wake up at sunrise like usual but several hours into the morning. There was a note slipped under the door from her lover who had come to visit after work. He forgot to write "Love" before his name. He had written "Sincerely" instead.

Settling down to a breakfast of milk and bread, the woman looked into the pot almost as an afterthought. Surely they would not survive the oven *and* the tires *and* the road. But. All seven—raw, gray, growing. Her mouth went dry, and she ignored them furiously for the rest of the day, jabbing the dirt with a spade as she bordered the house with nasturtium seeds.

Later that day, she stapled them in a box and lugged them to the post office and mailed them to Ireland, where potatoes belonged. She left no return address. When they were back in the pot the next morning, she soaked them in kerosene, lit them on fire, and kicked them into the hills. When they were back again the next morning, she walked two miles with them in her knapsack and threw them over the county line, into the next county. But they were back again by morning, and again, and again and again, and by the twentieth day, they curved inward even more and had grown sketches of hands and feet.

Her heart pulled its curtain as she held each potato up to the bare hanging lightbulb and looked at its hint of neck, its almost torso, its small backside. Each of the seven had ten very tiny indented toes and ten whispers of fingertips.

Trembling, she left the potatoes in the pot and fled her house as fast as she could. She found no comfort in the idea of seeing her sincere lover so she went to the town tavern and had a glass of beer. The bartender told her a long story about how his late wife had refused to say the word "love" in the house for fear she only had a certain amount of times in a life to say the word "love" and she did not want to ever use them up. "So she said she liked me, every day, over and over." He polished a wineglass with a dirty cloth. "I like you is not the same," he said. "It is not. On her deathbed even, she said 'Darling, I like you.' " He spit in the cloth and swept it around the stem. "You'd think," he said, "that even if her cocka-mamie idea were true, even if there were only a certain amount of loves allotted per person, you'd think she could've spent one of them then."

The woman sipped her beer as if it were tea.

"You say nothing," he said. "I don't know which is worse."

On the buzzy walk home, she stopped by the cemetery and on her way to see her family she passed the bartender's wife's grave which stated, simply, SHE WAS GREATLY LOVED.

Back at her house, holding her breath, she sliced all seven

potatoes up with a knife as fast as she could. The blade nearly snapped. She could hardly look at the chubby suggestions of arms and legs as she chopped, and cut her own finger by accident. Drunk and bleeding, she took the assortment of tuber pieces and threw them out the window. She only let out her breath when it was over.

One piece of potato was left on the cutting board, so she ate it, and for the rest of the evening she swept the stone floor of her house, pushing every speck of dirt out the door until the floor rang smooth.

She woke at the first light of day and ran into the kitchen and her heart clanged with utter despair and bizarre joy when she saw those seven wormy little bodies, whole, pressed pale gray against the black of the cast iron. Their toes one second larger. She brushed away the tears sliding down her nose and put a hand inside the pot, stroking their backsides.

In the distance, the sunflowers on the hill waved at her in fields of yellow fingers.

August came and went. The potatoes stayed. She could not stand to bother them anymore. By the fourth month, they were significantly larger and had a squareish box of a head with the faintest pale shutter of an eyelid.

Trucks, big and small, rattled through the town but they did not stop to either unload or load up. She hadn't seen her lover in months. She hadn't been to the cemetery either; the weeds on her family were probably ten feet high by now.

With summer fading from her kitchen window, the woman saw her neighbor meet up with the latest suitor, yellow petals peeking out from her wrists and collar, collecting in clusters at the nape of her neck. He himself was hidden by armfuls of red roses. They kissed in the middle of the dirt road.

Inside her house, the woman shivered. She did not like to look at so many flowers and the sky was overcast. Pluck, pluck, pluck, she thought. Her entire floor was so clean you could not feel a single grain when you walked across it with bare feet. She had mailed her electricity bill and bought enough butter and milk to last a week. The nasturtiums were watered.

The smacking sound kept going on by the window. Wet.

It was lunchtime by now, and she was hungry. And you can't just eat butter by itself.

She put the potatoes in the oven again. With their bellies and toes. With their large heads and slim shoulders. She let them bake for an hour and a half, until their skin was crisp and bright brown. Her stomach was churning and rose petals blew along the street as she sat herself down at her kitchen table. It was noon. She used salt and pepper and butter, and a fork and a knife, but they were so much larger now than your average potato, and they were no longer an abstract shape, and she hated potatoes, and the taste in her mouth felt like the kind of stale dirt that has lost its ability to grow anything. She shoved bite after bite into her teeth, to the sound of the neighbor laughing in her kitchen, through such dizziness she could hardly direct the fork into her mouth correctly. She chewed until the food gathered in the spittle at the corners of her lips, until she had finished one entire enormous potato. The other six crackled off the table and spilled onto the floor.

That night, she had a horrible stomachache, and she barely slept. She dreamed of a field of sunflowers and in each pollened center was the face of someone she once knew. Their eyes were closed.

At dawn, when she walked over to the stove, as she did every morning now, pulling her bathrobe tighter around her aching stomach, there were only six potatoes in the pot. Her body jerked in horror. She must have miscounted. She counted them over. Six. She counted again. Six. Again. Six. Six. Again. Six. Her throat closed up as she checked under the stove and behind the refrigerator and around the whole kitchen. Six. She checked all their markings until it was clear which one was missing: the one with the bumpiest head, with the potato eye right on its shoulder blade. She could feel it take shape again inside her mouth. A wave of nausea swept over her throat, and she spent the rest of the day in the corner of the old red couch, choking for breath. She threw up by evening from so much crying, but the seventh potato never came back.

The sunflower fields browned with autumn, and within a

month, two other potatoes were expelled from the pot. There was simply not enough room for all six in the pot anymore. She had done nothing this time. She didn't want to put them outside, bare, in the cold, so when they were soft enough, she buried them deep beneath the hibernating nasturtium seeds. They never came back either. The four remaining in the pot seemed to be growing fine but it was unsettling to look in and see only four now; she had grown so used to seven.

By the eighth month it was raining outside and she was having stomach cramps and the potatoes were fully formed, with nails and feet, with eyelids and ears, and potato knots all over their bodies. They rotated their position so that their heads faced the mouth of the pot. On the ninth month, they tumbled out of the pot on the date of their exact birthday, and began moving slowly across the floor. They were silent. They did not cry like regular babies and they smelled faintly of hash browns. She picked them up occasionally, when they stopped on the floor, legs and arms waving, but mostly she kept her distance. They tended to stick together, moving in a clump, opening their potato eyes to pupils the same color as the rest of them.

The four were similar, but you could distinguish them by the distribution of potato marks on their bodies, and so she named them One, Two, Three, and Four. Two also had a tiny wedge missing from its kneecap, in the shape of a cut square.

When she left to go mail a letter or pick up some groceries, the potato visitors went to the windows like dogs do, and watched her walk off. When she returned, they were back at the window, or still at the window, waiting. Their big potato heads turning as she walked up and opened the door. Eyes blinking fast to welcome her home. She went through her mail and fell into a corner of the rotting old red sofa and they walked over and put rough hands on her shoulders, her knees, her hair. The five of them spent the winter like that, together in the small house, watching the snow fall. She tried to send them outside, to find their fortune, but they always turned right around and came back. They only slept when she slept, making burbling noises like the sound of water warming up. They were dreamless, and woke once she awoke.

On the first day of spring, the bountiful neighbor came over with lilies woven into her hair, asking to borrow some matches. The woman had the four hide in the bathroom. She tried to talk to the neighbor but had very little to say and instead the neighbor filled the small house with chatter. The neighbor was in love! The neighbor liked the weather! The neighbor asked to use the bathroom and the woman said sorry, her bathroom was broken. The neighbor talked at length about broken bathrooms, and how difficult, and if she, the woman, ever needed to use her bathroom, she was welcome anytime. Thank you. You're welcome! When the neighbor left, the woman's ears were ringing. She went into the bathroom to pee and was somehow startled to see the four still in there, blinking beneath the silver towel rack.

"Get," she said, brushing them off. "Get away from me. Go!"

They bumped out the door and waited in the living room. She put them in the closet and went about her day, and there they stayed, waiting, until the guilt drove her to let them out. The following morning, after a sleepless night where they gazed at her with white pupils, she pushed them out the front door to the side of the house where there was a strip of dirt that the neighbor could not see. The woman picked up her gardening shovel and dug a hole in the earth, as deep as her knee. She looked at One.

"Get in," she said.

He stepped into the hole.

"Lie down," she said. He looked up at her with wondering eyes and she filled the hole with dirt over him.

"Go back to where you came from," she said, as she shoved more dirt over his grayish body. She looked at Two. Built another hole. "Go," she said, "and don't you come out," and her voice shook as she said it. Two hopped in without pause. As did Three and then Four. She filled the holes up fast and then strode into her house and locked the door. Fine, she said to herself. Fine. Fine. FINE. She ate dinner alone and slept alone and woke alone, and the cast-iron pot was empty when she checked. They wouldn't fit in it anymore anyway. She couldn't even eat them now, could she? They would just walk right out of the oven, right out of her mouth. Go back to where you came from, she told herself. Thank you, Goodbye, Excuse me. She swept endlessly, and trucks moved past her window.

In the morning, with spring rolling off the hillsides in bright puffs, she went outside to the strip of dirt. No movement at all. She set a rock at each site, one rock for One, two for Two, etc. She sat for long spells, over the course of the next week, and watched the sky drift overhead. It all felt very familiar, and she recognized the shape and texture of her life before, but it was as if someone had put her old life in the laundry and washed it wrong. The color was slightly off. The sleeves were now too short.

At the end of the week, she kicked off the stones and got out her big shovel. Her neighbor was hanging up clothing on her laundry line, green dresses and blue scarves. The wind whisked her hair around.

"How's that broken bathroom?" she yelled.

"Oh," said the woman. "Well. There never was any broken bathroom."

The neighbor raised her eyebrows.

"I was hiding my children from you," said our woman.

"Children? What children?" said the neighbor, wrapping

her neck in a rose-colored scarf. "I had no idea! How sweet! How many? Where are they?"

"I buried them," said the woman, waving her shovel.

"You what?"

"I buried them," said the woman. "And now I am going to dig them back up."

She went to the side of the house, and dug up One first. He sat right when the shovel touched his arm and dirt fell from his face and legs. He blinked at her, as if no time had passed at all, and she held out her hand and pulled him out. She dug up Three, and Four. She thought briefly of leaving Two there forever, letting weeds grow all over him, but the other three were looking at his spot expectantly, so she dug up Two too.

The woman looked at each in turn. The layers of dirt became them.

"Okay," she said.

They stepped into her open arms, solemn as monks. As they nestled and burrowed into her neck, the neighbor poked her head around corner of the house, draped in a clean sheet.

"Oh!" she said. "Look at this!"

The woman glanced over with Three on her back and Four clinging to her shoe.

"I didn't think you could be serious," said the neighbor.

"I am always serious," said our woman.

The neighbor crouched down and smiled at Four. "Are you okay, honey?" she asked. Four looked past the neighbor and then climbed onto our woman's back, pushing off One who fell lightly to the ground.

"They look so pale," said the neighbor, her voice unsure where to drop, into which voice box positioned between curiosity and righteousness. "You might want to call a doctor," she said. "I know a good one, who can be here within the hour."

Four curled his hand around our woman's neck, and began tugging on the lobe of her ear. Our woman barely smiled at her neighbor. It was a smile not made of pity, and it was not made of envy, even though the two had merged, for years now, on her lips. This smile instead was built of a weariness, of the particular quiet of the body after a long bout of weeping or illness. Certain things endured, and somehow she had ended up with four.

From the ground, Two leaped up to swing gently from her wrist.

"They need no doctors," she said, walking to her front door. "Trust me."

Inside, the woman dressed the group in clothing even though they had no hair or blood and would never look normal, dressed or undressed. Still she put them in pants and shirts she had sewn herself; in hats and shoes and belts.

She took their slow-moving hands and walked out the door again. They blinked and ducked under the lemony March sun. Already, like clockwork, the very first buds of green were pushing up from the soil, a ring of nasturtiums and dead potato babies to border her house. Halfway down the block, she turned and glanced at the neighbor, who was wearing a straw hat now, planting tomatoes. The four glanced with her. Thinking of the doctor had been a kind idea; she would thank the neighbor later. Living next to abundance was not so awful after all. It was contagious, in its own way.

The rest of the town was quiet and drowsy as the five walked past the cemetery, where they waved to the headstones, and over to the edge of the county. The air smelled ripe with spring. At the county line, the potato children stood by the fence posts and laid their hands on the dirt. They seemed interested, even pleased, by the new setting. They had no traumatic recollections of their past week buried alive. Instead, they brought fingers dusted with soil to their noses and smelled appreciatively.

They all crossed over, and began walking. A farmer pulling a wheelbarrow full of corn stopped and said hello.

"Good day," said the woman.

His eyes flicked to the bluish figures at her side, but he was a polite farmer and didn't say anything.

"How's the corn?"

"Fine," said the farmer. "Should be a good growing season. Good weather."

He kept his eyes steady on her face.

"These are my children," said the woman, giving him permission to look. "Children," she said, "say hello to the nice farmer." The four lifted their hands to touch him, and the farmer, familiar best with things of the earth, felt a wave of fluency, inexplicable, wash through him. His own son ran to catch up with them. "Here's mine," he said helplessly.

She shook the boy's hand, the boy who was fixed on looking at the potato children, and who, the way children do, immediately felt entitled to touch their nubbly elbows.

"Do they talk?" asked the boy, and the woman shook her head, no.

"Do they have magic powers?" asked the boy, and she shook her head again.

"They stay," she told the boy.

The farmer touched each potato child on the shoulder, and then waved goodbye to return to his work. He gave his son the day off. "Enjoy yourself," he said, surprised by the pang of longing in his voice. The group walked around the county, trailed by the farmer's boy; most things were very similar here except for the one movie theater showing a Western. In the interest of novelty, they all went to see it. The farmer's son ate popcorn. The cowboys rode along the prairie. There was a shoot-out at the saloon. The potato babies found it all amazing, and although they could not eat the popcorn, they clutched handfuls of it in their fat fingers until it dribbled in soft white shapes to the floor.

Afterward, the farmer's son ran home for dinner, and the

family of five crossed back over. The sky was darkening with clouds, and halfway home, it began to rain. The woman tried to huddle the four under her arms, but they resisted, and held their bodies freely under the water. They seemed to enjoy it, tilting their faces to the sky. She had never seen them wet before, and rain, falling on their dirty potato bodies, smelled just like Mother at the sink, washing. Mother, who had died so many years ago, now as vivid as actual, scrubbing potatoes at the kitchen sink before breakfast. How many times had she done that? Year after year after year. Lighting the new fire of the morning. Humming. Her skirt so easy on her waist. Her hands so confident at the sink. They were that memory, created. Holding their potato hands up, they let the rain pour down their potato arms, their potato knees and legs, and the woman breathed in the smell of them, over and over, as deeply as she could. For here was grandmother, greeting her grandchildren, gathering them in her arms, and covering their wide faces with kisses.

The *Case*

of the

Salt and

Pepper

Shakers

Let's face it. The dead bodies were clearly acts of easy murder, done by the husband to the wife, then the wife to the husband. I found them face-to-face, cold, on the living-room carpet. There is nothing here to solve. The only mystery I can see I have addressed in my report, which will soon be on the desk of my superior, and has to do with the number of salt and pepper shakers in a household of two people. Fourteen seems to me excessive. That, in my opinion, is the living core of this mystery. If you want a motive, I will write it out: the husband hated his wife because she had stopped speaking to him years ago; the wife hated the husband because he was stupid with their money. All this has been verified by various neighbors, relatives, and friends. No one I spoke to was particularly shocked by the double murder, seemingly planned on the same day which, if nothing else, seems to show a sense of kinship between the two. But! No one, including the neighbor, the doctor, and the bosses, understood why two people who paid a live-in chef to the very edge of their budget, and whose blood pressure kept climbing up the ladder into the red zone, would collect salt and pepper shakers, in ceramic, wood, glass, and metal. Does this mystery put anyone at risk? No. Will I get reprimanded again for not sticking to the outlines of the report? Of course. But I believe that mysteries surface in unexpected forms, and if I am to be a genuine investigator, then I must follow what I feel needs investigation.

I spent the night in their house staring at the rows of salt and pepper shakers while the bodies were being examined at the morgue. The cook was away for the night, and I slept in the guest bedroom, on top of the comforter, not moving any evidence but just resting and listening, as the only way to get a true feel of a house and its residents is to stay in it overnight. This model was fairly standard for the neighborhood: one story, ranch style, two bedrooms and an office. The pictures on the walls were restful landscapes, and in the guest room, I slept beneath a watercolor of horses running. Every piece of furniture and decor was slippery to the mind and would not stick. I can hardly recall the sofa or the chairs, so unobtrusive was their style, and so involved was I with examining those shakers. Several pairs were masterfully crafted, with zigzag patterns of mahogany and oak, or cut diamonds of crystal, and must have cost quite a pile. One was a humorous set, each a green ceramic frog: salt with a cane, pepper with a hat. Each held varying levels of grain. The house grew so quiet that I could hear the movement of cats next door, paws treading softly on the sidewalk.

In the morning, I awoke to a call from the coroner. He confirmed that the husband was knifed in the stomach at five P.M., while the wife had been poisoned at a quarter to three, with a poison that took exactly 2.5 hours to kick in. They both died within about a minute of each other. Her late lunch had been a small chicken potpie, unsalted, a green salad, peppered, and a glass of freshly squeezed grapefruit juice. He had skipped lunch, worried as he was about the exactitude of the poison, which he had slipped into her water bottle. Her fingertips, as she carefully cut and chewed her chicken and carrots, were covered with bandages from all the blade-checking she'd done over the course of the morning. She was described by several sources as a thorough type.

The coroner is an upstanding fellow. He fought in Vietnam and raises orchids. I thanked him repeatedly but he gets embarrassed by gratitude and hung up.

After I ordered in a bowl of tomato soup and a sandwich, I spent several hours in the living room, sitting with the stain from his wound. It spread over the carpet in a curling line, as if he'd put his arm around her with his blood.

Now, she could not have known she was poisoned when she knifed him, as he had chosen a poison that is silent and causes no suffering, and he had hidden the bottle somewhere very difficult to find, as we had not yet found it. In fact, their greatest difference was revealed through their choice of murder weapon, in that she wanted to make him suffer and be aware of her murderous inclinations, choosing the overt and physical technique, while he selected the secretive method, one of the few available where she would die without fully realizing what was happening. He perhaps was more ashamed of his loathing, and also he did not want her to feel pain. Their greatest similarity, however, was revealed in their choice of occasion, since each conceived of the exact month and moment of death fully independent of the other. Certainly that was something. And I imagine that as they lay on the carpet next to each other, one bleeding from the gut, the other foaming from the mouth, they saw something meaningful and linked in the eyes of the other. The nature of hate is as elusive as love's. I for one am just pleased they did not have children.

Back to the dilemma of the spices. I finished my lunch and

called up both their hairdressers, and spoke to one very un-friendly sibling, and no one had any interest in discussing these salt and pepper shakers, and in fact I could feel a stirring annoyance in the voices of the questioned, one which I am used to but still resent. I went home to shower, and spoke briefly with my girlfriend who was half asleep, and seemed dis-tracted, and only right before I dozed off in my own bed did a phone call come in and tell me that the missing bottle of poi-son had been discovered in the chef's quarters, underneath her bathroom sink. Curious. I had not met her yet; she had taken off several days to grieve, and was returning the follow-ing morning to begin the slow process of packing up her bags. This couple had not been exceedingly wealthy, but the luxury of a live-in cook was something both felt was important to their happiness. So they shared a car, and rarely ate out or va-cationed.

I found the cook in the kitchen, making afternoon snacks. Nothing was packed yet, and the house was just as I had left it. The couple had been married for twenty-five years and the cook was older than I expected, with a head of silver hair, al-though her fingers were still swift and nimble. She seemed saddened by the loss of her employers, but perhaps not sad enough. I was not ready to rule her out as a possible accomplice, particularly now with that poison bottle, wrapped in plastic, sitting bulbous atop the coroner's desk. While we were talking she made us a perfect turkey sandwich, on a triangle of bread, grilled lightly on the stove.

"The wife liked salt and the husband liked pepper," she said, "and the salt and pepper pair served as a symbol of their relationship." She briskly flipped the sandwich on the grill and then scooped it onto one yellow plate and one red plate which she handed over to me.

"Thank you," I said. The bread had crisped to a fine golden color around the edges. I waited until she took a bite of hers until I tried mine. "How so?"

"Well," she said, swallowing carefully, "they used salt and pepper as their model ideal. In their wedding vows, they said she was salt–she intensified the existing flavor–and he was pepper–he added a new kick–and that every fine table needed both.

"In fact," she said, leaning in, "instead of a man and woman atop their wedding cake, they had a pair of miniature salt and pepper shakers."

"No kidding," I mumbled, chewing.

She nodded. "I can show you photos." She started toward the living room, and before I could take another bite, she had the white wedding album open, full of smiling attractive faces, and there was the cake, with those shakers on top. "It was a white cake with strawberry cream filling," she said. "Quite light."

"Did you have any reason to dislike either one of them?" I asked casually. "Were they good employers?"

"Yes," she said. "I liked them just fine. Isn't the case solved?"

"Seems to be," I said. "It's just that no one else remembered the shakers." I tried to keep sandwich crumbs off the photos. "This is delicious, by the way."

She shrugged. "I've been here since the wedding," she said, pointing to herself with a full head of very brown hair in the photo album, serving plates of cake, "and that was their gift to each other every single anniversary."

She shut the book. "Case closed," she said.

I opened the book back up. "Except," I said, pointing to the date on the invitation, "there are only fourteen pairs of shakers, and I believe they were married for twenty-five years . . ."

"Twenty-six," she said, pulling a clear bag of lemons up from the floor. "Well.

"What happened," the cook said, now slicing lemons in half, "was that after about fourteen years of marriage, he, as people do, grew sensitive to spicy food, and her blood pressure went up so high that she had to abandon salt. She could only use pepper, he only salt. He did not like the salt, it seemed to him redundant, which hurt her feelings. She did not like the pepper, as it seemed to distract from the true nature of the dish. This made him feel discounted.

"After some time, she grew less vibrant, and he less stimulating."

"Truly?"

"From my perspective," said the cook, "it actually seemed to be true."

I pressed my finger into the plate to pick up the last crumbs of sandwich.

"And did this fill you with a strange hatred?" I asked.

She smiled at me. "No," she said. "Why, you don't believe they killed each other?"

"We found the bottle of poison in your room," I said.

She sat back down in her chair. I said nothing. At moments like this, it is always best to say nothing. Her eyes faded and lost focus.

"I'm not so surprised," she said softly after a while. "I'm sure he put it there on purpose. He had always hoped that I would be able to fix it all. I tried," she said. "It is a chef's job, this," she said, squeezing lemon juice into a pitcher.

She sighed now, with some elegance in her shoulders, and stirred the growing pitcher of lemonade with a wooden spoon.

"But a good chef must let go of the salt/pepper ratios," she said. "It's uncontrollable. It is a chef's nightmare to see the saltshaker dump itself all over a perfectly salted piece of meat or to see the pepper dirty up what is an ideal wave of béchamel. It is a chef's sleeplessness, right there," she said.

"So let it go," she said. "I cannot worry about it excessively. I simply Can Not." She poured herself half a glass of lemonade and took a sip. "Too sweet," she said, cutting four more lemons precisely in half. "And if lemonade is too sweet," she said, "then we are somehow lost to the crush of anonymity."

Her face struck against itself, and her eyebrows folded in.

"Sir," she said, "I was here for twenty-six years. Had they trusted my expertise, perhaps none of this would have happened."

I found I wanted to comfort her but her eyes had shut down, and after I finished spiking the last crumb, I tried to thank her sincerely, but she had lost herself in thought, at the kitchen table, stirring four grains of sugar at a time into the pitcher, and tasting, repeatedly, with the large wooden spoon.

"Thank you for your time," I said, then, to no one.

It was not the chef. I believed her fully. The evidence was in. But if the mystery was solved, both big and small, then why was I still on it? That was what my boss kept asking over and over. He had a new case for me. This one involved a homicide on the west end of town, of a very old rich codger who had seven children and it seemed likely that one of the seven had killed him. But I was bored by that one. It will solve itself, like a hose releasing its pinch and letting the water flow. I bought some orchid food instead and went to see the coroner again, because my mind would not stop thinking of that end, when the husband and wife realized they were dying together, each by the hand of the other. In a way, they actually had swapped personalities, by killing the other in the manner of his or her favorite spice. The wife chose knifing, which is certainly "pepperlike" in its spicy attack on the body, and the coroner thanked me for the orchid food and confirmed my suspicions about the poison, by explaining how the one the husband had chosen killed by increasing the saline level of the bloodstream to such a degree that the person essentially dehydrated.

I myself have a girlfriend, as I have mentioned, which is perhaps why the salt and pepper pair do not leave my mind. The case is closed and the file cabinet locked but I still think of them all the time. The ranch-style house sold for cheap to a small family who moved here from Michigan and didn't hear the history. I believe the chef retired from family work, and now is doing private catering on her own, and if I ever get married, I will surely hire her, although my superstitious girl-friend might not approve. I do love my girlfriend, for her differences and her similarities, but I do not know if one day the item that defines me in her eyes will no longer work. If my body will fail. If I will face her in bed and not know what to do, when now her body still seems infinite. If she will stop having that bright look in her eye at the parrot store, and instead lose herself circling letters in word searches. There are couples who commit suicide together and they are in line with Shakespeare's greatest lovers, but those who murder each other precisely at the same minute are written up in all the papers as crazy. Even their family members coughed and got off the phone as fast as they could. They would like to erase the whole rigamarole. I picked up more than one tone of disgust and superiority in my many interviews. But it seems to me beautiful. How right at the end, when everything was over, they realized they had reached the ultimate gesture of compromise, that their union had come full circle, and perhaps it was the sting of that bittersweetness that killed them most, crueler than any knife or poison.

The Leading Man

The boy was born with fingers shaped like keys. All except one, the pinkie on the right hand, had sharp ridges running along the inner length, and a point at the tip. They were made of flesh, with nerves and pores, but of a tougher texture, more hardened and specific. As a child, the boy had a difficult time learning to hold a pen and use scissors, but he was resilient and figured out his own method fast enough. His true task was to find the nine doors.

• • •

Door one he found as a kid; it was his front-door key. He did not expect this because it seemed so obvious but one day he came home from school and was locked out; his mother, usually home, had just begun taking some kind of sculpture class and was off molding clay and forgot to leave a key under the welcome mat. So he was unwelcome, in his own home. He cried for a bit and tromped on some pansies as revenge and got so frustrated staring at the lock, such a simple piece of metal separating him from his palace of food and bed and TV and telephone, that he stuck the index finger of his right hand inside. It shoved deep into the lock, bumping around, trying to find a perfect spatial match. Nothing clicked. But he'd enjoyed the sensation so he tried the middle finger next. Too big. The pinkie on the left hand: too small; it wiggled inside like a wire. It was the ring finger on his right hand that slipped inside, easy as a glove, ridges filling the humps and the boy settled it deep, rotated his entire hand, heard the click, and the door opened cleanly. Inside. He ripped his finger from the door and let out some kind of vicious delighted laugh.

When his mother came home, two hours later, hands red with clay, he pulled her straight to the door and showed her the trick. Shove in, turn, click, open. His mother kept laughing. And I didn't even want to buy this house! she said, holding him close. And to imagine, what if we hadn't?

The boy shrugged. He had no idea how to answer that question.

The second key fit the lock of the bank deposit box that held all the securities of the family. The two had gone on a trip to the bank and the boy was bored in the room of security boxes while his mother spoke worriedly with an accountant. He stuck the pinkie on his left hand into their security box and ta da. He was very surprised. So was his mother. I didn't especially like this bank either, she said. Can I have some of this money? the boy asked, looking with interest at the large piece of gold sitting in the box like a glowing turd. No, she said, but I'll buy you a burger. They went to his favorite burger joint where the lettuce was shredded and the soda ice crushed, and she told him about how she was making a clay version of him. It's you, she said, but you are surrounded by doors. You are standing on doors and wearing doors and your hand of keys is held up like a deck of cards. The boy splayed his fingers out on the table. Gin, he said.

The third, fourth, and fifth keys opened his camp trunk, the neighbor's car, and the storage room of the school cafeteria, respectively. He opened the cafeteria door one day at school when he was wandering around, not wanting to go home yet because there was nothing to do and no one to be with. All the other kids were off playing sports. The boy opened the back of the cafeteria with his right pointer, to his own almost dulled surprise, and sat with the frozen chicken nuggets for a while. It got boring quickly so he went home, opened the door with his other finger, and watched TV. His father was away at war. No one knew what war it was because it was an unannounced war, which made it worse because he could tell no one because that would cause great governmental problems. So he just held on to that information and when his friends asked where his dad was on Open House Night at school, he said, He's away on business. He wanted to yell out, The business of saving everyone's life! but he knew that would cause further questions so he kept his mouth shut.

His mother brought home the clay sculpture. It was about two feet tall and looked very little like him, and the doors resembled flying walls. One day when he was home alone and she wasn't back yet, having enrolled in another course, this one called How to Make Glass, he threw some baseballs at the sculpture but the clay held strong. The boy was twelve now. His hands were growing, but his fingers still fit the same locks.

Somehow they stayed the size they needed to be, while the rest of the hand–palm, knuckles, wrist–grew with him.

The sixth and seventh keys fit doors in France. His mother and he went to Paris to visit his father who was on leave from the mysterious war and together the three of them had lunch at a café surrounded by iron lamp poles and they ate crusty bread and soft cheese with red ripe tomatoes. His father looked older and stronger than ever, with big arms and a ruddy tan, and the boy stood next to him and wanted to push all his keys at once into the man's palm, to click and turn his father open, to make him tell what was happening. Secrets. His father and mother shared a room in the hotel and the boy had the room next door, with its strange-smelling comforter and a weird phone that had numbers in different configurations. He learned how to say *Ou est la porte?* which means Where is the door? and the porter at the hotel, after ignoring the question for the first five times, finally showed him a door, standing alone, on the lobby level, hoping to shut the boy up. Using the middle finger on his left hand, the boy opened to reveal just a closet, empty, with a few clothes hanging up and several swinging hangers. The porter babbled in amazement, *Mais qu'est-ce que c'est que ça?!* and took one of the hanging shirts straight away to the maitre d' at the restaurant who had been bemoaning the loss of it for more than a year and the boy said, to no one, I suppose I'm just going to sit here, and he went inside the closet and curled up on the floor. The porter, when he returned, brought the boy a glass of wine and a piece of apple. When his mother found him, asleep on the floor of the closet, she hugged him for a long time, and he showed her how his hand was international.

At the Louvre, the boy felt the pointer finger on his left hand itch after greeting Mona Lisa under glass. He found the docent room the way a hound finds blood, and played gin rummy with a pooped guide whose earrings were little diamond stars. His father was off doing military business that day. When they returned to the hotel, the mother angry at the boy because he'd vanished, they found the father weary on the bed, looking worried, his ruddy tan fading like a bright couch left too long in the sun.

On the airplane home, the mother cried and the boy went to the bathroom and thought of his father as he peed, and then when he flushed he sent his pee like a message to his father because he imagined it flying out of the plane, free of him, into the world.

Go win the war, the boy thought, and come home. Or, he thought, don't win the war and come home. Or, he thought, don't come home but make Mother stop missing you. Or, he thought, make me stop missing you.

He rubbed his keys against his palm. He was almost thirteen. He washed his hands with the lavender airplane soap and returned to his seat.

He didn't fit his eighth key until he was twenty years old.

His father did come back from the war after another year, but he was not the same man. He was scared of noises and he had a strange white blindness that he experienced when the day got too hot. The family considered moving, over and over, to cooler quarters; considered it, then unconsidered it. The boy took drama classes but always played the funny weird guy and never the leading man. He watched his mother take How to Make Glass II, the second in the series of five, and one afternoon she came home with a tote bag full of huge clear squares. She said this was her final exam for the class, and she'd gotten an A. Look, she said, pointing, no bubbles, she said. The boy asked her what they should do with it now that she'd made it. She said break it. So they took it outside and broke it in two and then his mother looked sad and sat down and the boy broke it in four, then eight, then sixteen, and his mother was still sad, she started to weep, softly, and the boy shattered the glass into hundreds of pieces.

His first girlfriend bought the chastity belt as a joke. He couldn't open it. They scrambled around, used the tin key that it came packaged with, opened her up, had sex anyway. Her underwear was thin and full of holes and the boy kept it that night in his bed, after they had parted, and thought about the way she butted her head into his shoulder like a goat. When they broke up, he walked to the bank and put the underwear in the safe deposit box right on top of that one piece of gold. His mother never said a word about it. The bank had changed ownership by now and had a new color scheme—navy and dark green—but the lock was exactly the same.

His father went to the hospital for the blindness. He told the doctor that he saw whiteness everywhere, as if he'd been driving in the snow for days and days, and that he couldn't find his balance or his peace. The hospital gave him painkillers and sunglasses. The boy's father sat in the kitchen with a cup of milk in a mug, his palm covering the opening so he wouldn't have to look at its white flat top and he said, It's not like I saw anything that horrible. The son said, Really? and the father said, Son, the truth is I can't even quite remember what I saw. Is it bright in here? he asked. The son looked outside at the setting sun and the lucid calm of dusk.

The eighth key fit the cabinet at a weaponry store. He went there for his college war survey class to learn the difference between muskets and spears. The man who owned the weapon store had a big belly and cheeks stretched over his face like poorly upholstered furniture. He would be hard to make in clay. The man was reading a book called *How to Meet Girls*, and when the boy asked to see some stuff, the man said he'd lost the key to the back cabinet where the small revolvers lived. The boy felt his finger itching, walked over, and opened it himself. The man's cheeks raised a full inch on his face, furniture renewal. The boy shot some targets and felt like a soldier and wrote a brilliant report. He read *How to Meet Girls* cover to cover.

His mother came to his college graduation. His father could not because the light of the sun blinded him and seeing people all dressed in one kind of uniform reminded him of the army and made his head feel like it would explode. I can't stand it, he told his son. All those bodies on the lawn in black graduation gowns. It's like one huge goddamn foxhole. His mother wore a dress she'd made in her sewing class, with contrasting patches of velvet, burlap, silk.

He went to France for a graduation present. He returned to the Louvre, deciding he wanted to play more gin rummy. He located the door, but when he stuck his finger in the lock, it didn't fit anymore. They had apparently changed locks since his last visit. This made him feel unsettled, as if kicked out of his own home. He wondered if that finger would find a new lock now. He thought: Yes. And no. And I don't know.

He met a French girl named Sophie, sitting in a yellow-and-brown wicker chair at a café, eating a butter-and-sugar crepe. He fell in love with her within a couple of days. She puffed her lips when she spoke, like the French do. In bed, he put his finger inside of her, the ring finger on his left hand, the finger that means marriage, as if to turn her inside and unlock her body. She came fast; she was loose and loving, and loud, and luscious, but she hadn't been locked, either. I love you, she told him, after a week, with a thick French accent, lips puffing. He decided to stay for the rest of August. They made love all the time and he told her his "uncle" couldn't see because he'd watched bad things in the war and Sophie said,

What war? and the boy shook his head. I don't know, he said. Some war somewhere kind of near here.

When he left France, Sophie said she'd write but she only sent one letter total. He returned to his hometown and found an apartment near his mother and father. He went to the man, still sitting around the kitchen.

Do you know who were you fighting? he asked.

Some other guy, said his father, stirring his tea.

What did you see? asked his son.

Not much, said his father. Some blood, he said. I think something got taken away from me, his father said. I think they took something from me but I never even felt it happen when they did.

The boy placed his right hand of keys into his father's open palm: the security box, the neighbor's car, the closet in France, the docent room at the Louvre that had been changed.

You say you've opened eight so far? said his father. Which is the ninth?

The son waggled his ring finger on his left hand. Well, go open some doors, his father said, squeezing his hand. The one you open with the ninth key will be connected to the woman you will marry. Maybe.

The boy took his hand back, and agreed that would be very sweet, if it worked out like that. He had been feeling a vague dissatisfaction at the mundane nature of the other eight keys. There was a report on the news that NASA had lost the key to the space shuttle, and so the boy called up right away and offered his assistance. The whole flight over he had the national anthem singing in his head. NASA took him straightaway to a sealed white room with serious people who shook his hand and had fierce eye contact, and members of the FBI lined the walls in case he was a terrorist in disguise. The boy tried all his fingers twice but none worked. The NASA people shook their heads, and he heard someone say, I told you so. He had a fleeting feeling of terror that the FBI might arrest him for something his father had done and an even bigger wish that an FBI man would arrest him, take him aside, and tell him what had happened. What is the greatest mystery of your family? he asked the older lady on the flight home, as they watched the movie without sound, and she looked at him thoughtfully but never answered. At home, he shoved his finger into every door he could see for a few weeks, but decided to stop, as it was starting to make him unhappy, and signed himself up for a sculpture class.

In the second class in the series on figure sculpture, the boy met a woman he wanted to marry. After a year, they married. They spent the gold piece in the safe deposit box on the wedding and did it up, and also did it dark so that his father could stand it. It was a night wedding. His father stood at the microphone and made a toast with his eyes closed. The son danced with his bride, luminous in her white dress; his father never once looked at the bride for fear his head would explode. That night, in the hotel room, the bride looked at the ring on his key finger and asked him what that one opened and he said he didn't know. They made love in the big hotel bed with the strange-smelling comforter and fell asleep face-to-face, feet tangled together.

They went to Paris on their honeymoon and found the closet in the hotel that the boy, now a man, could open, and when the porter wasn't looking, they snuck inside and made love. Due to the intrusion of the walls, sex was uncomfortable in the closet, so they ended up going to the front desk and getting a room anyway. There, on the bed in the hotel, the man told his new wife about his father and the war. He told her everything he knew which was very little but still, other than the quick "uncle" confession to Sophie, he'd never told anyone. He had to continually smother down a fear of the FBI busting into the wiretapped room and taking him to FBI jail as he spoke. The new wife was understanding but equally confused. We were at war then? she said. The man said, You are the first person I have ever really told. Her face was dim in the light of Parisian dusk, filtering through the windows and turning the room golden. He felt glad he'd married her. They went downstairs and had a feast of duck in apricot sauce in the hotel dining room and the porter, who was now significantly older, recognized him and gave him a free crème brûlée. After dinner, the porter insisted he open the closet again, which he did, with embarrassment, because to him it still smelled like his wife's desire and not like an abandoned closet in the least.

They found a good apartment in town, near his parents. They got a dog at the pound who had been abused but was responsive. His mother came over with teas from around the world and sat at the kitchen table in her patchwork outfits, and she and the dog got along. The son still tried to ask his father the right question that would reveal everything but all he ever got in reply was a sad shaking of the head.

On his thirtieth birthday, he was walking to work, to the factory where he broke glass for a living, when he heard screaming in the streets. He passed a TV in a bar, and the local news was explaining how a little boy was locked in a metal shed by accident and the door was too thick and couldn't be banged down. The young man took a detour on his route and went toward the noise and the banging. Apparently the boy had been in the shed for hours and air would run out soon. This was a special boy too—the one known about town whose

elbows were pointed in such a way that made it easy to open
tin cans.

As he approached, the crowd, who knew him well, parted
willingly when they saw him walking over. He could hear the
boy inside the metal room, sobbing up the air. The young man
with the hands of keys paused a moment in front of the metal
door. He could feel his finger itching. He wanted to wait for a
second and hold this moment, the moment before he became
a finite person. He could feel the air ringing with it—his life
span a life span, the world a round ball. The crowd screamed
and the boy sobbed and the young man put the ring finger on
his left hand in the lock.

Click.

Hero.

The trapped boy ran out crying, gasping, elbows in wings,
and the town lifted the young man with the key fingers on

their shoulders and they wrote headlines and gave him a medal and the mayor shook his now-complete hand.

After the award ceremony, he went to his parents' house. His father was sleeping in a quiet dim room, and the young man slipped the medal over his father's head. He'd passed many doors that day and thought: so I can't open that one or that one or that one. From now on, all the doors in the world were as closed to him as to everyone else. The older man kept sleeping and the young man hummed a song to himself inside the cool dark room.

Hymn

The unusual births hit the town all at once. All the mothers, not recognizing their babies. Mine is so tall! said one, craning her neck. Mine so blond, said the dark next, squinting. Mine made of paper, announced a fleshy third. Mine built of glass? trembled another. One with a child who had no eyes, but ears so acute they could measure blinking. Another with a daughter who could, at will, turn into objects like brooms and light-bulbs. Soon, at the playground, the children could not recognize what made the other work, and they eyed one another from behind the swings, from beneath the tire sculpture.

When they were older, they took over the village and ran it perfectly. Little did their mothers and fathers know. That when they'd eaten the foods and breathed the air and felt the feelings and made the love that created their children, they were, for once, in perfect synchronization. The son of glass was a doctor, and all could see inside his body while he worked on theirs. The daughter of paper was a scholar, and each book became a part of her wrist and arm and breast. The blond son lit the town for those months when electricity was no longer an option, and the daughter of great height cooled the moon with streams of her breath when it grew too hot from a passing meteor.

The changeable woman was always on hand to provide the most needed machine or tool. The child with divine ears listened to the soil, and pointed to where he heard the seeds unfurling with pleasure. Plant here, he told the one with the longest arms who could reach straight into the heart of the dirt. In later years, that eyeless one sat beneath the forest of trees he could not see but could take deep inside his lungs, and when the sadness was unbearable, it was only he who could soothe the villagers. Who could hear the type of tears by the pace of the blinking, and know in which manner to offer comfort.

Their parents were gone by then. The world had fallen into sense and sorrow.

Mother, they said. Father.

This is our decision, they said, bowing to each other.

Once a year they stood together, holding hands as best they could, with the new babies crawling on the floor at their feet: the babies of many heads, the ones made of words, the clay blobs. The triplets of air who would rush past and sweeten your breathing. Who's that strange one you made, Ma? Why, Pa. That creature is your own flesh and blood. Even though it has neither flesh nor blood; still, it is yours.

Then the grand feast, with food of all kinds, even for the several who did not eat food but survived only on the quality of listening. They usually hovered at the corners and when they grew wan and skinny, it was a reminder. To focus. On this day, they filled up visibly, fat and happy.

No one needed to say it, but the room overflowed with that sort of blessing. The combination of loss and abundance. The abundance that has no guilt. The loss that has no fix. The simple tiredness that is not weary. The hope not built on blindness.

I am the drying meadow; you the unspoken apology; he is the fluctuating distance between mother and son; she is the first gesture that creates a quiet that is full enough to make the baby sleep.

My genes, my love, are rubber bands and rope; make yourself a structure you can live inside.

Amen.

Acknowledgments

Much gratitude to the support and wisdom of Suzanne, Karen, Meri, and David Bender, with a special nod to Suzanne for the good kick-in-the-butt talk; the excellent editors of the journals and magazines that published these stories and others; the Corporation at Yaddo; Jennifer Carlson; Rolph Blythe; Kendra Harpster; Jeanne Leary; Danielle Adler; Ryan Boudinot; Bernard Cooper; Lori Yeghiayan; Eric Welch and IW; Phil Hay; the great Julie Newman from before and great Julie Reed now; the terrific Henry Dunow and inspiring Bill Thomas; and the continually vital readerandfriendships of Miranda Hoffman Jung, Alice Sebold, and Glen Gold.

ALSO BY AIMEE BENDER